CHRISTMAS AT THE
WARATAH INN

LILLY MIRREN

Black Lab Press

THE WARATAH INN SERIES

The Waratah Inn
One Summer in Italy
The Summer Sisters

Christmas at the Waratah Inn
(a standalone novel)

10TH DECEMBER 1996

DEE WHY

Elizabeth Cranwell was re-evaluating her life choices. Specifically, the one that resulted in her running alongside the Dee Why lagoon, puffing and wheezing behind her gazelle-like friend, Ivy.

Flanked on one side by squat residential housing, brick walls in various shades of red and brown, tiled roofs, and tidy timber-slat fencing, she fixed her eyes on the skyline ahead, focusing on each laboured breath as it burst from her lungs.

"Almost there!" trilled Ivy with a glance and smile over her shoulder in Liz's direction.

Liz couldn't manage more than an *oomph* in response.

She was forty-seven years old. When would society allow her to simply give up on these attempts at athleticism? She hadn't been an athlete in her twenties, and she highly doubted it would happen now.

She tried to say something to that effect, but the wind whipped the words from her mouth and flung them over her shoulder to where Margot huffed behind her. At least she wasn't as unfit as Margot. That thought dragged a slight smile to the corners of her mouth for a moment, until the beginnings of a stitch twinged on one side of her ribcage, and she grimaced.

The breeze that fluttered over the lagoon cooled her as it lifted the lank hair from her neck. It wasn't really a lagoon but more of an inlet of sea water that had nowhere to go. A trio of pelicans floated on the lagoon's surface. One propelled itself forward with strong rhythmic beats of two webbed feet beneath the water's surface, sending ripples fanning out in the blue ahead of it.

She focused on the pelicans and the blue sky overhead. She noted that there weren't many clouds, then pivoted to thoughts about how that wasn't good news for farmers who'd been suffering under a drought for the better part of five years. Still, she mused, it was a pretty day.

Anything to keep her legs stumbling forward and her mind off the possibility that her heart might explode in her chest at any moment.

She couldn't stop now. Ivy would never let her live it down. She'd blame the donuts, the white bread, the crispy chips, and they'd never hear the end of it. No, that wouldn't do. Liz would simply have to keep pushing forward.

She shot Margot a sympathetic look. Her friend's face was a study in red; sweat poured down either side of it. Her lips were pursed, and she squinted into the morning sun.

"Whose...idea... was this?" grunted Margot, between gulped breaths.

Liz arched an eyebrow. "I thought it was yours."

"Next time, shoot me," replied Margot.

Liz chuckled then groaned at the growing pain in her

side. She could see the headland and could glimpse the ocean. Not far now. She squeezed her eyes shut and focused on each step, each breath. She could do it. She slammed into Ivy's back.

"What are you doing?" croaked Ivy, staggering forward.

Liz's eyes flitted open, and she caught herself before plunging headfirst into the pavement. "Oh, sorry. I was focusing."

"Next time focus with your eyes open," complained Ivy, rubbing her back.

Liz stood with her hands on her knees, gasping in air for a few moments until her pulse slowed to a more normal pace, then straightened to take in the view. It really was beautiful.

Waves curled in slow motion, drawing toward the shore. Sunlight glinted off the azure waters. Seagulls circled and cawed nearby, and green shrubbery clung to the hillside that curved down from where they stood to the beach below.

Margot sat on the footpath; her eyes dull. "Maybe next time we should think about going to a cafe to catch up."

Ivy laughed, stretching one foot up behind her until it tapped her taut rear as she raised an arm to counterbalance. "No, this is perfect. I love it out here. So beautiful, and look, the sun is already getting high in the sky. Dawn is the best time to be outside at this time of year."

Liz walked to the railing that ran around the headland and leaned her elbows on the timber. She adjusted her sunglasses and breathed in the sea air. It was almost worth the pain.

Almost.

Ivy joined her. "What are you doing for Christmas this year?"

"Um... not sure yet. You?"

Ivy shrugged. "Steve and I are going to visit the kids." All three of Ivy's grown children lived in the Blue Mountains where Ivy and Steve had raised them. The two of them had decided to move somewhere warmer after their children, who she still called *the kids,* left home.

"That sounds nice."

"Will you visit David or Danita?" asked Ivy.

Liz's son, David, was studying architecture in Melbourne and her daughter, Danita lived in London, and worked for a large accounting firm there. She hadn't seen either of her children in months and was trying hard not to feel blue about it. David had only left home that year to attend university. She'd been hoping he'd pick a school in Sydney, but he'd chosen to move interstate, leaving her alone in the big and now very quiet house where she'd raised them.

"I haven't spoken to David about Christmas yet. I'm assuming he'll come here, but Danita's going skiing with a group of friends in Austria, so I won't be able to see her this year for Christmas I'm afraid. As you know, Mum and Dad are in Cairns, and I would visit them but they're going on some kind of safari..."

Margot slipped into the space between Liz and Ivy. She struggled to get one foot up onto the railing, then proceeded to stretch her leg, both hands angling toward her upturned foot, her face contorted. "I'm sorry to hear that, Liz." She grunted then exhaled a sharp breath. "At least you have David."

Liz nodded. At least she had her son. Her husband was an entirely different matter. Ex-husband now—she still hadn't gotten used to saying it. After all, they'd been married for twenty-three years, separated for two and divorced for one. It was hard to believe it was over, that she was a single woman in her late forties. She'd never thought she'd find herself in that situation, because they'd been the couple everyone knew would last.

They'd even built an architecture firm together. *Cranwell Design* had a stellar reputation around Sydney. They'd worked together and raised a family together over two decades, and now he was living with the woman she'd hired as her associate.

"What will you do this year?" Liz asked Margot.

Margot smiled. "We're flying to New Zealand to see Frank's family. But we're headed back the day after Christmas. Can't stay too long, things get a bit heated on that side of the family I'm afraid. Frank is keen to come home and relax for the new year before we both have to head back to work."

By the time she'd caught her breath, Liz was dismayed to see Ivy jogging back in the direction they'd come. With a groan, she pushed her tired legs to follow her friend. At least there'd be steaming hot coffee and croissants when they got there. It was her favourite part of their weekly catch up.

❦

THE WARM WATER IN THE OVERSIZED TUB LAPPED AT LIZ'S chin. Bubbles foamed and fizzed around her as the bath bomb she'd thrown into the water offered its final gasp, sending pink bath salts spinning through the water. She squeezed her eyes shut and leaned her head back on the folded towel she'd placed on the edge of the tub.

It was nice to finally have some time to herself. Time to relax after all these years. She'd raised a family, built a business, and now she was free to do what she wanted with her days.

Still, since it wasn't exactly her choice to be retired at the grand old age of forty-seven, her newfound freedom was bittersweet.

She and Cameron hadn't only gotten divorced a year earlier they'd also dissolved their business partnership. The successful architecture firm they'd built together over many years of hard work, turmoil, heartbreak, and several near bankruptcies, was no more. Cam had chosen his new girl-friend over Liz, and he'd decided that working with his ex-wife wasn't fair on the new girlfriend. Especially since the girlfriend was one of Liz's employees. Now, he had his own firm, with the girlfriend working alongside him as Liz had done for all those years.

Liz sighed and blinked her eyes open. She turned the hot tap on with one toe, letting more hot water into the tub. It pummelled her feet, and she groaned as the stiffness from their run earlier that morning worked its way through her tired muscles. She didn't feel middle-aged most of the time, but Ivy had a knack for bringing it out in her, especially when she made them run, rock climb, mountain climb, or any other of the myriad adventures she took them on, calling them opportunities to grow.

Liz shook her head. She was grateful for both her friends, even if Ivy did put her life in danger with such regularity. In truth, if it hadn't been for Ivy and Margot, she wasn't sure she'd have even left the house during the past two years.

Claws tapped on the hardwood floors in a steady rhythm, getting louder as they approached. A large, brown head appeared through the bathroom door, and a pink tongue lolled out of the corner of Macy's mouth.

"Macy girl, come here."

The chocolate Labrador happily trotted to the side of the bathtub, tail wagging. Liz stroked the animal's head with one wet hand.

"If it wasn't for you and the girls, I don't know where I'd be right now," murmured Liz.

Macy licked her arm, her tail thumping against the tiles.

The phone rang, jangling in the bedroom and set Liz's heart racing. She climbed out of the tub, wrapped a towel around her still dripping wet body, and hurried to answer it.

"Hello?" She dabbed at her hair with the end of the towel.

"Hi, Mum," said David.

She smiled, always happy to hear his voice. It'd been hard letting him go; he'd always been her baby, always so close to her. He'd been the child who'd clung to her on the first day of kindergarten, unwilling to let go. Now she felt like that child, not wanting to release her grip on him as he went off into the world, now a young man. He'd gone without a backward glance, as he should. And she'd had to remind herself every day that she'd done her job as a mother when she saw how independent he'd become. Still, she missed having him hover around her as a child, asking a million questions, or sitting on her lap peppering her face with sweet kisses.

"Darling, it's good to hear from you. How's uni?"

He grunted. "It's fine. Still there. Hey, I wanted to talk to you about Christmas."

A frown creased her brow. "Okay."

He cleared his throat. "Brianna wants me to meet her parents..." His latest girlfriend had featured in every telephone call for the past three months. It wasn't a surprise to her that things might be heating up between the two of them. Her eyes narrowed. "That's nice."

"So, we're going to spend Christmas in Tasmania... you know, with her mum and dad."

Liz's heart contracted. "Oh."

"Sorry, Mum, I know how much you love Christmas and everything. It's just that she really wants to take me to her parents' farm, show me around, introduce me to the family... you know how it is. We'll come up to Sydney next Christmas. Okay?"

She exhaled the breath she'd been holding in her throat. "Next Christmas? That sounds serious."

He laughed. "Yeah, I guess so. Look, I've gotta go, Mum. Love you."

"Love you too."

He hung up and Liz stood there, dripping onto the hardwood floors, staring at the handpiece. She swallowed hard. He wasn't coming home for Christmas. Neither was Danita. Cam had moved on and would no doubt be spending the holiday with his new girlfriend and her family. And she would be here, in this big, airy house, all alone.

She glanced around the master suite. Perfectly decorated in creams and tans with azure blue accents. A dormer window with a window seat and perfectly placed throw pillows, curtains that draped on either side of it, positioned to let the natural light in. A king-size bed, neatly made, with a large acrylic painting of a beach scene poised above it.

She'd spent so much time making her home exactly what she thought a home should be. She'd designed it herself, sketched out the floor plan more than twenty years earlier on her drafting table into the wee hours of the night as her eldest slept in a cot down the hall of their tiny apartment. It was their dream home, her and Cam's. And now every footstep she took echoed a hollow thud through its long, empty hallways. Every cough or word she spoke hung in the vaulted ceilings. What was the point of having such a house if it was empty of love, of laughter, of family?

Tears filled the corners of her eyes. She dried off, pushing the lump that'd formed in her throat back down as best she could. Then she dressed in a pair of navy-blue slacks with a cream blouse. She blow-dried her hair, her throat still tight. She wouldn't let this derail her. She'd come so far already this year. The divorce had sucked the air right out of her lungs, especially when Cam had brought his girlfriend to the solicitor's office to discuss the division of assets. She'd barely been able to raise her gaze from the table in front of her, willing herself not to cry, not to shout, scream, or rant about the unfairness of him leaving her right when she was done raising his children and building his business.

Liz inhaled slowly, sucking air into her aching lungs. She set her hairbrush down on the vanity and took one last look at her reflection in the mirror. Shoulder length, light-brown hair with blonde highlights, green eyes, a smattering of fine lines around their corners, and full, pink lips perfectly painted.

She'd done everything right. How had she ended up in this place—alone at Christmas?

Ever since her business dissolved, she'd struggled to find things to do with her days. Eventually she'd return to work, maybe find an architecture firm and interview for a job. The idea made her shudder, she'd been her own boss for so many years, so would she be able to fit in somewhere else?

Today she was going Christmas shopping with Margot and Ivy. They'd agreed to do it weeks ago when her friends had dropped by the house late in the afternoon, and she was still moping around the house in her pyjamas, eating ice cream from the container with a spoon.

The Audi's engine roared to life and Liz backed out of the three-car garage and down the long, curving driveway. It was only a ten-minute drive to the shopping centre, and she found a parking space without much difficulty. These were the things that occupied her thoughts now: clothing, traffic, parking spaces, and which shade of lipstick would best match her accessories. The absurdity of it made her stomach churn.

She'd been a successful entrepreneur, a businesswoman, a mother, a wife... and now, what was she? She honestly couldn't say. Who was she? She didn't know.

She met Margot and Ivy in front of Myer and pushed a smile onto her face.

Ivy wore long, black leggings paired with a flowing silk shirt that reached almost to her knees. Her golden hair was pulled back into a sleek ponytail. Margot wore jeans and a t-shirt with a black jacket, sleeves rolled up to her elbows. Her brown curls fell untamed across her forehead and into dark eyes.

"Hey, there you are. We were about to send out a search party," said Margot, offering Liz a hug.

Liz grunted. "Sorry, I had a phone call that... kind of threw me."

"What happened?" asked Margot, concern darkening her eyes.

"David called. He's not coming home for Christmas."

"What?" Lines creased Ivy's forehead. "What happened? Is he okay?"

Liz sighed and stepped forward, urging her friends to walk with her. She didn't want to disrupt their shopping trip with more bad news. It seemed she'd had nothing but complaints to offer to her friends in recent months. She was sick of the sound of her own voice.

She ran a hand over her hair, smoothing it into place. "He's going to Tasmania with his girlfriend. They're spending the holidays with her parents."

Margot huffed with her eyebrows pulled low. "I'm so sorry, honey. That really stinks."

"I don't know why he doesn't consider your feelings," responded Ivy, eyes flashing. "What is it with our children? Everything's about them."

"He doesn't think about it because he's never had to before," replied Liz with a sigh. She stopped in front of a window and studied her reflection in the glass. Sadness pulled down the corners of her mouth. She used to smile all the time.

Margot's arms crept around Liz's shoulders and her friend squeezed gently. "I'm sure he didn't mean to hurt you."

"He didn't. And to be fair, it's not his responsibility to

make me happy. I can't expect him to give up his life because mine is empty." She issued a hollow laugh. "He should go and have fun with his girlfriend. What I really need to do is stop waiting around for my children to visit me, and get my own life."

Ivy shook her head. "You have your own life."

"Do I? I don't know anymore." A lump formed in Liz's throat.

"You should go on a cruise or something," said Margot, resolve hardening her voice. "Yes, you should do something completely out of character. As you said, you can't wait around for other people to fill the void, you've got to take action."

"Well, I don't know if I meant that..." Liz's eyes widened. She'd never considered taking a cruise at Christmas. The holidays were a time to spend with family, not to lay on the deck of a boat alone in your swimsuit. Weren't they?

"Look, there's a cruise line right there." Margot pointed and Liz's gaze followed her direction. They were standing in front of a travel agency. Posters advertising azure waters, golden beaches, and tanned bikini-clad women enjoying these exotic locations lined the walls.

"I have no desire to lay on a beach by myself somewhere romantic..." Before she could finish her sentence, Margot had grabbed her by the hand and pulled her into the shop.

"Come on, let's see what they have," said Margot.

Liz stumbled after her, eyebrows lowered. "This is not helping."

Ivy followed after them, spinning slowly as she walked, taking in the plethora of images offering happiness and perfection. "I wish we weren't going to the Blue Mountains... I could do with a beach holiday."

"Newsflash Ivy, you live at the beach," grumbled Liz, crossing her arms over her chest.

Ivy laughed. "Good point. So, why don't we ever enjoy it then? I think going away somewhere is important, even if you already live by a beautiful beach. Somewhere else is always more relaxing. Don't you think?"

"I guess." Honestly the last thing she wanted to do was go somewhere alone at the holidays. It'd simply draw attention to the fact that she had no one to share Christmas with. Her friends meant well, but the idea didn't appeal.

"Can I help you?" A young woman with long, brown hair that shone under the bright, fluorescent lights smiled at them, red lips revealing large, white teeth.

"Yes, you can," replied Margot with an equally white grin. "My friend here is looking for somewhere to spend Christmas... somewhere exciting..."

"Relaxing," added Liz with a flare of her nostrils. In fact, she hadn't agreed to go anywhere at all, but at least they should get one thing straight, adventure did not agree with her. She'd learned that the hard way when Cam took her tramping along the Milford Track in New Zealand and she'd not only twisted her ankle but almost ended up with frostbite in her toes and fingers which the doctors at the time had said was almost unheard of for that time of year. The fact was, she wasn't the adventurous type, she was a stroll along the beach, sit by the pool, and sip Mai-Tai cocktails kind of woman.

"I have something I think will be perfect for you. We've been getting some great feedback about the Waratah Inn on the coast of northern New South Wales. It's just had a complete overhaul and it's really very beautiful," said the woman, pulling a brochure from a stand behind her and handing it to Liz.

Liz studied it and her brow furrowed. It did look nice. The photographs of the inn showed a building with historic charm, surrounded by beautiful flower beds and tall gum trees. When she opened the brochure there were images of an idyllic, deserted beach and people riding horses over the sand.

"Horse riding?" she asked, offering the brochure to Ivy to take a look.

"You've always wanted to do that," replied Ivy.

Liz nodded. "I guess it doesn't seem so bad..."

"Not so bad?" exclaimed Margot, shaking her head. She stepped in front of Liz and took hold of both Liz's arms, fixing her eyes on her friends. "This is perfect for you. I couldn't go to New Zealand thinking you're stuck in that big house all alone at Christmas. Please, do this for yourself, for us. We'll be worried sick otherwise. And who knows, maybe you'll even have fun."

2

11TH DECEMBER 1996

SAINT LUCIA, QLD

Robert Patch scanned the rows of students' faces as he finished up his class. The words didn't require much thought these days, he'd been teaching biology for so long that the lessons were almost automatic, though he always tried to inject new life into the subject. Not that it seemed to matter. Almost every student in the room seemed to be suffering from some level of coma-like boredom. The room swam with warmth and lazy yawns.

First-year students. They were always the most difficult to engage. Some hadn't decided yet what they'd study and were trying out biology as a prospect. There were too many students in the room as well, something he'd mentioned more than once to the department head, but it didn't matter — the university had bills to pay and first year students helped to keep the lights on.

"Thanks everyone. That's all for today. I'll see some of you next year in Advanced Biology. In the meantime, have a wonderful Christmas and I'll see you next semester."

Suddenly everyone in the room became animated and alive again. They leapt to their feet, smiles crossed faces, conversations buzzed.

Inside he sighed, he did his best, but the fact was, young adults simply weren't particularly interested in bacteria or DNA. At least, they certainly didn't seem to be. Or maybe it was his voice, he'd always been told it had a soothing quality. Probably not the best for teaching.

Still, he loved to teach. It was one of the few things left in his life that brought him pleasure. Especially when he saw the looks of boredom on the faces of his first-year students turn to curiosity as the year progressed, and then excitement when he asked them to swab each other's hands for bacteria and identify what they found under the microscope. It was a fun icebreaker that usually weeded out those who were genuinely interested in the study of biology and those who were simply doing it for school credit.

As the students filed out of the room, laughing and chattering, he packed up his notes and tidied the room ready for the next lecture. He didn't usually teach during the summer semester, preferring to keep it free for research, but had agreed to cover a few classes for a colleague who'd recently had her appendix removed. Today was his last day of teaching for the year and he was ready for the break.

It'd been ten years since he'd accepted the job at the University of Queensland. Ten years since he lost his wife Martha to cancer and left Townsville for Brisbane to start a new life. It'd seemed like the right thing to do at the time given the fact that their only daughter lived nearby on the Gold Coast.

He sighed and ran his fingers through his hair, then

tucked his briefcase beneath his arm and headed out of the room. The science building was one of the oldest at the university. Long dark hallways, spacious lecture rooms with hard, timber, stadium-style seating and rectangular windows running along one wall.

"Have a good Christmas!" called Bill, a colleague from the physics department. He held a leather briefcase beneath his arm, waved a hand in the air.

Rob nodded in his direction. "You too, Bill. You headed up to Rainbow Beach?"

"Yep. We're staying at the cottage for a full month. I can't wait." Bill and his wife Sue often went up north to a fishing cottage they'd bought years earlier. They'd never had children, so Christmas was a lonely time for the two of them until they'd decided to embrace it. They'd bought the cottage and spent a lot of time on the banks of Tin Can Bay.

"Don't catch too many fish, make sure you leave some of them in the ocean for the rest of us."

Bill laughed, pushed a large pair of black rimmed spectacles up the bridge of his nose. "I can't make any promises. See you later."

Rob waved goodbye. The hallway was dotted with students, all on their way to somewhere. He was done for the day, and usually he'd head back to the teacher's lounge for a quiet coffee with some of his colleagues. But today, he wanted to get home as quickly as possible. He had a phone call to make and he couldn't put it off any longer.

He waved goodbye to a few familiar faces as he went, striding forward at a steady pace. The university campus was a large one and parking was at a premium. He'd left his car at home and instead rode his bicycle to the nearby campus. He unlocked the bike, tucked his pants leg into his socks, to keep from getting grease on them from the chain, tugged his helmet onto his head, and climbed onto the bike.

The side-eye he got from students passing by didn't faze him. He didn't care if he was fashionable, not anymore. Those days were behind him. Now, all that mattered was his daughter and grandchildren. What they thought, and how he could be part of their lives was the most important thing to him. Them and his Golden Retriever, Rocco.

Rob pushed forward on the pedals, slow at first, then set a steady pace. The traffic was light, and the day hot, though the worst of it had passed. Summer in Brisbane was stifling, and leaving the air-conditioned classroom to ride home, even with the sun dipping toward the horizon, felt as though he'd stepped into an oven and had the door swing shut behind him. Still, he loved the vigour of it after a long day of teaching or sitting behind his desk to mark exams or assignments. And the feel of the wind on his face.

His house was narrow at the front. It stretched along a thin block of land that bent over one side of a hill. Traffic crept by, clogged at a nearby roundabout. Rob sailed past on his bicycle, climbed off in the driveway, and parked beside his small, yellow hatchback.

Inside, claws scratched a hasty path to the front door before he'd had a chance to throw his keys in the fish-shaped bowl on the entry table. Rocco launched himself at Rob, tail thumping against Rob's thigh as the animal turned first one way, then the other, keening all the while.

Rob laughed. "Yes, I'm home. It's good to see you too, boy." He stroked Rocco's side, then tousled his ears.

A mirror hung over the entry table and Rob caught a glimpse of himself. His sandy blond curls had been flattened by the helmet and beads of sweat had curved narrow streams down both sides of his face. His blue button-down shirt had pools of wet ballooning from beneath each arm.

He turned on the thermostat and listened for a moment as the air-conditioning whirred into action. Then, he descended the narrow, timber staircase to his bedroom. The house had been designed in the modern open-plan style with dark browns accentuated by pale creams. Since it stepped down a sloping block, his living area and kitchen occupied the top floor, and the bedrooms, rumpus room, and home gymnasium took up the bottom floor, before opening out through wide, concertina glass doors to the base of a tall oak tree. He had no yard to speak of, only a small patch of grass that Rocco frequented, and that Rob didn't clean up as often as he should.

Rocco padded along the hall behind Rob, his tail still happily wagging, and his breath puffing hot against the back of Rob's pants.

Rob undressed while he walked, tugging the damp shirt free and fanning it to let some air find his skin.

In his room, the phone on the bedside table jangled, startling him for a moment. One of the unexpected consequences of losing his wife ten years earlier to cancer had been the fact that his phone hardly ever rung anymore. It turned out that his entire social life had been wrapped up in his wife and her friends, and once she was gone it wasn't long before those friends moved on, and he was left on his own, attempting to pull the remaining shreds of his life back together. It'd been hard at first, wondering where everyone was, what they were doing, why they hadn't called. Why was it so quiet all the time? Why didn't the phone ring anymore?

Now he was used to it. So used to it, that the sound of the phone startled him with its unfamiliar tone. The only person he spoke to on that phone was his daughter, and he always called her, not the other way around. Rocco stared at the contraption with a look of bewilderment on his face that mirrored Rob's own.

Rob quirked an eyebrow. "I'm as surprised as you are.

Must be a telemarketer. Though even they don't seem to call these days."

He threw his soiled shirt into the clothes hamper inside the walk-in closet, then picked up the phone.

"Hello."

"Dad?"

The sound of Jennifer's voice brought a smile to his face. "Jen, how are you?"

Her voice brightened. "I'm fine, thanks Dad. What are you up to?"

He tucked the phone beneath one ear, cupping it in place with his shoulder as he worked his way out of his pants. An immediate relief, he sighed as the cooler air soothed his sweat-dampened skin.

"Just got home from work, love. How about you?"

"I'm cooking dinner. Listen, Dad..."

His eyes narrowed. Whenever she said that, something was coming she knew he wouldn't like.

"You know how I said you should stay here for Christmas? But then we talked about how it might be better if it's just a lunch thing..?"

He nodded. "Uh huh."

"Well, since our house is so small, there isn't a lot of room. And Neil's parents will be dropping in as well, maybe his sister and her kids... Neil thinks we should stick with lunch. I know I said I'd talk to him about it..."

"I was really looking forward to staying, so I could spend more time with you..." Rob squeezed his eyes shut, shook his head.

"I know, Dad. I was too... I'm sorry." Her voice softened to a whisper. "Neil thinks..."

"Neil thinks I shouldn't stay?"

Jen fell silent. In the background a television set blared.

"Okay... well, that's fine." Frustration twisted in Rob's gut.

He'd tried so hard to like Neil over the years, done his best to accept the man who'd married his daughter, as a son. But every year that passed made it more and more difficult to pretend that things between them were good... or even cordial.

Jen cleared her throat; he could hear her drawing in a deep breath. "What I'm saying is, it's going to be busy, and the house is cramped already with Neil and the kids... I have a lot on my plate. Neil thinks it might be too much for me..."

"Don't you mean too much for him?" retorted Rob, biting his tongue to keep from saying more.

Jennifer hesitated. "Again...I'm sorry, Dad. The kids and I wanted you to be here. I think it's best..." The shine had gone from her voice, it was soft, broken, full of hidden tears.

He sighed, softened by her tone. "Yes, of course love, I understand. It's a lot. Christmas can be a stressful time for everyone. Don't worry about me, I'll get a hotel room or something. I want to spend Christmas with you, and I can be flexible. After all, I don't have to accommodate anyone but myself."

He knew how hard it was for her. It still made him angry when it seemed she wouldn't stand up to her husband. He pushed her around and she wouldn't fight back. Surely if she stood her ground... He ran a hand through his hair. He didn't understand it and could never comprehend how his beautiful, intelligent, carefree, and confident daughter had ended up with a husband like Neil.

"Thanks Dad. I'm sure Neil will be fine with that. We can even sneak out to see you as well."

He didn't respond. What could he say? *Why do you feel the need to sneak out of the house with the children to visit your own father?* It wouldn't help her, wouldn't make her feel any better.

What he really wanted to do was visit Neil in the middle of the night with one of his golf clubs. The nine iron might do the trick. Though of course Rob hadn't been violent a day of his life. He'd never even fought with his brothers growing up. He'd been the bookish one, the boy everyone else got along with. The peacemaker. He'd never felt the need to use force to get his way. Until now. Now he wished he'd been the forceful type, learned how to push his weight around. He wished he knew how to stand up to a bully like Neil without endangering his daughter and grandchildren.

They talked together a few more minutes before he hung up, then he stood still, staring through the open blinds at the back yard. The dying sun danced on the surface of the glass outdoor table, sending shards of light through the window to shimmer like rainbows across his bed.

3

21ST DECEMBER 1996

CABARITA BEACH

The yellow cab rattled as it bounced over a pothole. Sea grass blew in the breeze, pulling away from the ocean as it glimmered and shone in glimpses between clumps of pandanus trees. The highway was narrow and straight, and Liz clutched her handbag tighter with fisted hands as they thudded over another pothole.

She fingered the seam on her purse as she stared out the dusty window. Seagulls angled away from the beach, wings beating a rhythm, their calls unable to be heard from inside the cab. She wasn't sure what to expect of the Waratah Inn. The brochure had made it look idyllic, but she was experienced enough to know that looks could be deceiving.

David and Danita had been supportive of the trip. Both had expressed their remorse at leaving her on her own over the holidays, but she'd assured them she'd be fine. She would be, of course. She had to be. There was an entire future, the rest of her life, to learn to be alone, so she might as well get started.

She had never spent Christmas alone before. Not once in her forty-seven years of life. Her childhood had been a happy one and she had fond memories of holidays spent with a large extended family. Then, she'd married Cam and they'd begun new traditions, new routines with a budding family of their own.

In fact, this was the first time she'd gone on holiday by herself. The spectre of lonely days ahead made her stomach churn. What would she do with her days? Usually, she busied herself taking care of others: cooking, cleaning, decorating, working hard to ensure everyone enjoyed the holiday. This year she hadn't bothered to get a Christmas tree. The house had looked depressingly plain when she stepped into the airport taxi. No twinkle lights, ornaments, or tinsel. Only bright heat glancing off the Colorbond roof.

The taxi pulled off the main road, tyres crackling on gravel. A pale-yellow building rose against a backdrop of gum trees and pandanus ahead. It had a warm, welcoming feel to it. White shutters, white verandahs, with brightly coloured flowers adorning the garden that spanned the outside of the structure, and in pots dotted here and there.

"Here we are," said the taxi driver, who'd been silent for most of the trip.

He helped her with her luggage and as she stepped through the front door, the scent of baking bread and other treats filled her nostrils and her stomach twisted with hunger. She hadn't eaten at the airport or on the flight—nerves had stolen her appetite—but it rushed back now as the delicious scents enveloped her.

Behind an antique timber reception lectern, a young woman with a sandy-blonde ponytail was checking in a guest. The guest looked to be about Liz's age, maybe a few years older. He had blondish curls infused with streaks of grey, kind, brown eyes, and wore clothes that didn't quite match but that gave him an endearing look that turned up the corners of her mouth in the first smile she'd managed all day.

She stood behind him to wait her turn. He fussed with a briefcase and a small suitcase. The woman behind the counter waited patiently for him to finish what he was doing, then he moved to one side, apologising softly with a glance over his shoulder at Liz. The look on his face tore at her heartstrings. His expression mirrored her own inner turmoil, perhaps he was alone as well.

He set his room key on the side of the lectern and continued to dig in his briefcase.

She smiled. "Never mind, take your time. I'm in no hurry."

He caught her eye, this time holding her gaze for several long moments. "Thanks."

She nodded, then focused her attention on the woman. Her heart skipped a beat and sweat beaded on her forehead. He really was very handsome, not something she generally noticed these days. She inhaled a slow breath.

"Hi, I'm Bindi, are you checking in?" asked the woman, a wide smile splitting her face and making her look about twelve years old. Though, in truth, everyone looked young to Liz these days, she never could tell whether someone was a teenager or in their twenties anymore, they all appeared childlike. And when she caught her own reflection in the mirror, she barely recognised herself.

"Yes, I'm Elizabeth Cranwell," she smiled her reply.

The woman scanned a ledger, then ticked something with

a pencil. "Ah yes, here you are. Welcome to the Waratah Inn, Mrs. Cranwell. It's our pleasure to host you this Christmas. You're in room eight, it's on the third floor. Jack here will take your bags up for you." Bindi indicated an older man who tipped his hat as he reached for Liz's bag.

"Thank you," she said.

Bindi handed Liz a key with a room number attached to it. Liz took the key. "Thank you, I'm looking forward to it." The knot in her stomach turned over. Looking forward to it wasn't exactly the right phrase. Perhaps if she said it out loud, it'd help her to see things differently.

That's what Margot had told her. It's all about your attitude, she'd said. If you go into it believing it's going to be fun, that you'll have a good time, you will. If you're dreading it, you'll have a lousy time. Simple.

Liz wasn't sure it was quite so simple as that, though she was desperate enough to try anything. Positive thoughts, encouraging words, she could do that.

Beside her, the man who'd checked in ahead of her was scanning through a stack of brochures. There was one about a river cruise that caught her eye. She set down her key and reached for it, opening it up to study the images of happy couples dining on board a river boat. She grimaced. She'd never noticed before how many couples there were in the world until she wasn't a part of one any longer.

Never mind, she'd have to get used to it, and this was a good place to start. She tucked the brochure into her purse, smiled at Bindi, and reached for her key. Then she climbed the stairs to the third floor. By the time she got there, puffing, she thought again that perhaps Ivy had a point about exercise after all. She should do more of it, and these days she really had none of the excuses of her past. No children keeping her busy, no career taking up all hours of the day and night. She could go to the gym in the middle of the day, if she wanted to.

The inn was bigger on the inside than it had appeared from the outside. A large chandelier hung over the staircase, and sunlight glinted from the shards of crystal flinging lights onto the pale-yellow walls. Tastefully selected pieces of furniture that reflected the inn's heritage in a modern way dotted the floor. She found her room without any trouble, noting that the man from downstairs was in the room right next to hers.

Her cheeks flushed with warmth as she pushed the key into the keyhole. It didn't fit.

Great. She'd have to go back downstairs and up again, by the time this day was over she'd have done more than her fair share of exercise. She spun on her heel and braced herself, then noticed the man beside her struggling with his key in the same way.

She glanced down at her key; the room number that dangled from it read 'nine'.

"Excuse me," she said, moving toward him and holding out the key. "I think somehow we've ended up with each other's keys. I'm in room eight, but I have the key for room nine, which I believe is yours."

He glanced up at her, eyebrows arched in surprise. "Oh?"

He looked at his own key then shook his head slowly. "How strange, I have the key for room eight. You're right. I wonder how that happened."

He smiled at her. His brown eyes were soft and reminded her of Macy's. She missed her dog already, though she knew how much Macy loved the pet retreat and was no doubt running and playing in a field with a dozen other dogs at that moment.

She handed him her key and took the one he offered. "Thank you. I'm Elizabeth."

"I'm Rob, pleased to meet you. At least I didn't have to walk all the way back down those stairs," he indicated the staircase with a dip of his head in that direction.

She laughed. "I know exactly what you mean. I was contemplating sliding down the bannister."

He chuckled. "Sounds fun. Maybe we can do that later."

Inside her room, Liz found the single small suitcase Jack had taken upstairs for her. Sunlight streamed in through windows that ran along one wall. A king-sized bed was set in the centre of the room with a colourful painting hung over it. Everything in the room was tasteful, welcoming, and stylish. Something Liz always appreciated. As an architect, she had an eye for these things. Decorating was something of a hobby for her, one she'd indulged over the years in her own home. Something that seemed rather pointless in hindsight, given the fact that the only people who ever saw it, other than her, were Ivy and Margot.

Since he'd moved to Melbourne to study, David had only been home once for a brief visit over the winter break. She'd thought he'd spend every holiday with her, but was making friendships, building a life for himself, and she couldn't expect him to hurry home every chance he got. It was a hard thing for her to accept, but denial was what had gotten her here in the first place. She'd known Cameron was having an affair for years before she finally confronted him, but by then it was too late for them to work things out. If she hadn't lived in denial, maybe things could've turned out differently. If she'd faced the fact that they were losing their connection, maybe he wouldn't have strayed.

Margot told her she couldn't think that way. That Cam was simply a cad, a sleazy, cheating low life. But Liz couldn't see him that way. He was the man she'd fallen in love with and together they'd raised two children. At first, she'd blamed him entirely, but lately... she could see it might've been partly her fault. Perhaps if she'd done things differently or treated him better...

She sighed and set her purse on the bedside table. There was no point in thinking that way. He was gone, the children had moved out of home, and this phase of her life wasn't turning out in the least the way she'd planned.

4

Rob lay on the bed, his stockinged feet crossed at the ankle and stared out the open window. Gum branches swayed in the breeze, and a lone kookaburra laughed in the distance. His room was comfortable if a little modern for his taste.

He sighed.

It felt strange to stay at a bed and breakfast over Christmas, alone. It was at times like this he missed Martha more than ever. After a decade of living alone, he'd grown accustomed to it. But holidays reminded him of what he no longer had. She would have loved this place.

When cancer stole her from him all those years ago, he'd thought that he couldn't possibly build something for himself out of the ashes of his grief. And yet, he was still moving forward. Sometimes it seemed as though no time at all had passed, and other times he could barely remember what they'd shared together. When he pictured her throwing back her head to laugh, her dark bobbed hair swinging around her ears, it seemed more like a dream than a memory.

Jennifer lived about a fifteen-minute drive from the

Waratah Inn. He could've stayed somewhere closer, but he had chosen a place as remote as he could find. He didn't like the bright lights and crowded streets of the Gold Coast. And so far, the inn was exactly what he'd hoped it would be. He always felt somehow out of place when surrounded by stylish people or decor. Martha used to laugh at him when he complained about it, telling him most people enjoyed nice things, but his eccentricities were the reason she'd fallen in love with him. Then she'd sit in his lap, curl her arms around his neck and kiss him softly on the lips.

Rob ran fingers over his lips now, struggling to remember how it'd felt. If he'd known then those kisses wouldn't last forever, he'd have savoured them more.

He didn't much enjoy watching television, so wasn't sure what to do with himself once he'd unpacked his bag and put everything away in its place. He stood with his hands on his hips surveying the room. He'd left Rocco with a neighbour, a woman who seemed to love his dog almost as much as he did, and who Rocco had escaped to visit on more than one occasion. Still, perhaps he should call her to check on him. No, he'd be fine. He was a dog. He was likely being spoiled beyond repair at that very moment.

"Right," he said to himself. "Downstairs."

He found a woman in the kitchen, stirring something in a pot over the stove. She had wide hips and an even wider smile. Her grey curls were damp with sweat, poking out beneath a skull cap.

"Well, hello there," she said. "I'm Jemima Everest, but you can call me Mima." Jemima Everest was a rotund older woman with salt and pepper curls that crowded her face, and striking blue eyes flanked by laugh lines that deepened the wider her smile grew.

"Hi, I'm Rob. Pleased to meet you."

"And you. Can I help you with anything, Rob?"

He shook his head and plunged both hands into his pockets. "Not really. Trying to get my bearings, figure out what to do with myself, really."

She chuckled. "I understand. If you like, I can tell you about some of the things we've got on offer here at the inn, see if anything tickles your fancy?"

He nodded.

"We've got horse riding along the beach, or you can walk on any number of trails around the inn, just get a map from the front desk. Also, there's a bus that comes by and picks people up to go to Tweed Heads, in case you feel like shopping..."

He shook his head. Shopping was one of the things he avoided until it was absolutely necessary.

"You staying for Christmas?" asked Mima.

"Yes, and for a few days after."

"Wonderful. I'm filling in for the chef while she's away, and I'm planning out the menu for Christmas lunch. Are you a ham or turkey lover?"

He quirked an eyebrow. "I like both."

"Both. Good idea. Let's have both. Why not?" Her eyes twinkled.

"You're not the chef?" he asked.

She shook her head. "Not anymore. It got a bit much for me. But I fill in every now and then, when they need me."

"That sounds like a good deal."

She nodded. "I love this place, couldn't imagine walking away from it entirely."

He felt the same way about the university. Sometimes he thought he'd never retire. What would his life be like without those dank halls and dusty classrooms filled with eager young faces? He couldn't picture it.

He explored the ground floor of the inn, found a small enclosed patio where a few people were sitting around eating scones and biscuits, with cups of tea. Then he wandered into a large sitting room. One entire wall was covered in book-shelves and books of every type graced its shelves. He ran a finger over the spines, reading each title until he found a thriller that looked like it would be to his taste. He carried the book to an armchair and sank into it with a sigh, flipping the book open.

He read the first paragraph five times before he realised it was hopeless and gave up. He couldn't concentrate. All he could think about was Jennifer and the kids, Sophie and Daniel. Why wouldn't Neil let him stay at the house? All that malarkey about the house being too full, too busy at the holidays was nothing but nonsense.

He couldn't say that to Jennifer, of course. She had to live with the man, a fact that stirred anger in his gut. She'd married him right after her mother died and he'd been too mired in grief to object much. Though he'd expressed his concerns over one dinner together. She'd brushed it off, telling him they were in love, and it'd be fine. He was different with her, she'd said. No one else got to see that side of him the way she did. With her he was considerate, gentle, loving, kind.

Just remembering made his blood boil. It turned out she was wrong. Neil was exactly the kind of man Rob had thought he was, and his kind, gentle treatment of Jennifer had ended the moment she said, "I do". Rob only hoped he treated the children better, though since he hardly got to see them, he had no way of knowing.

He should go over there, spend some time with them. Surely Neil couldn't object to that. It was almost Christmas after all, and he'd come here for that purpose. He'd stop by the bakery on his way over there, bring some Danish pastries or vanilla slice. Vanilla slice had always been Jen's favourite when she was a kid, and even though so much had changed since then, he hoped that hadn't.

He flipped through the pages of the book, studying the paper. How many people had read this book before him? About to begin the same paragraph over, he was distracted by someone else entering the sitting room. When he looked up, he saw it was Elizabeth, the woman he'd met earlier. There was something about her that caught his attention. Something in her eyes, her demeanour. A sadness combined with a regal poise.

She was beautiful, of course, he'd noticed that right away, but his attraction was more than that. She was vulnerable, hiding it behind a mask of confidence. He wanted to hold her and tell her everything would work out okay in the end, not a feeling he was accustomed to having. He'd never been the knight in shining armour type.

"Hello again, Elizabeth," he said.

She smiled, but the gesture didn't make it to her eyes. "Hi, please call me Liz. I hope I'm not disturbing you. I thought I might try to find a book to read and Bindi said I should look in here."

He held up his book. "I had the same idea."

"What are you reading?" She took the seat next to his and leaned forward, crossing one long leg over the other and smoothing the crease in her slacks.

"I don't know... some kind of thriller."

She laughed. "It's obviously making an impression."

He shrugged. "I can't get into it. Too much on my mind."

"I know the feeling."

"Are you here for Christmas as well?" he asked.

She nodded. "Yes, I'm staying for about a week."

"Me too. Mima tells me she has a delicious Christmas lunch planned..."

A look he couldn't decipher flashed across Liz's face. "That sounds fine."

"Though, of course, you might have other plans, I shouldn't assume..."

She inhaled a sharp breath. "No. I don't have other plans. Nothing at all."

It was hard for him to believe a woman like Elizabeth Cranwell had no one in her life to spend the holidays with. What had happened to leave her alone at this time of the year? Although in fairness, he hadn't expected to find himself in the position he was in at this stage in his life either—if he wasn't entirely alone, it felt that way. Pity stirred in his heart.

"I'm sorry, I shouldn't have said anything."

She pushed a smile onto her face. "No, it's fine. I have to face it sometime. I'm alone at Christmas." She issued a hollow laugh. "How horrible that sounds."

"It's not so bad," he quipped. "I have to spend Christmas with my son-in-law. Trust me, alone is better than that."

Her eyes narrowed. "Really?"

"I couldn't miss seeing my daughter and grandchildren though. So, I play nice. Otherwise I might not get to spend time with them at all."

She quirked an eyebrow. "You don't look old enough to have grandchildren."

He laughed. "Really? I feel it. We were married young and had our daughter right away. Funny thing is, we only ever wanted one child. My wife and I agreed on that, if nothing else. And we doted on her. Probably too much."

He shook his head. If he could do things over, what would he change? He'd done the best he could at the time. He knew what Martha would say, that Jen's choices were her own, that he couldn't control her and that what she did was no reflection on his parenting. Still, he couldn't help wondering if spoiling her had led her to marry a man like Neil.

Liz smiled and nodded as he spoke. She gave him her full attention, her blue eyes fixed on his. Warmth flooded through him.

"I'm going out today, but I was thinking of taking a walk along the beach tomorrow afternoon. Would you care to join me?" The words were out before he'd thought them through. It wasn't like him to be so forward.

Her cheeks flushed pink. "Actually... that sounds lovely."

THE PACKAGE OF VANILLA SLICE NESTLED IN ONE HAND, A bag holding bottles of chocolate milk in the other, Rob strode down the front path toward his daughter's single-story red brick house.

It'd been months since he'd seen them. Weeds had grown taller than the plants in the garden bed and choked them out. The ground was dry and dusty, the lawn pockmarked with bare patches where the grass had died. Kids' tricycles and other toys were scattered across the yard.

A frown creased his brow. It wasn't like Jen to let things get out of hand around the house that way. She'd always been a neat freak, so everything had its place; she loved a tidy house. After Martha died, she'd come over regularly to clean up after him when he hadn't been able to summon the strength or the motivation to do it. That is, until Neil came along. After that, everything changed.

He raised a fist and knocked on the weathered timber door. A dog barked in the distance. A bead of sweat trickled down one side of his face. When the door opened, Neil leaned against the doorframe and stared at him with a hollow smile.

"Rob, good to see you."

Rob cocked his head to one side, held out a hand to shake Neil's. "Always a pleasure, Neil."

"Come on in." Neil stepped aside, but his presence loomed as though challenging Rob to push back. Neil was tall, with dark hair and eyes shadowed by dark smudges. Broad shoulders tapered to a narrow waist and thin legs poked out, hairy beneath a pair of rugby shorts.

Rob stepped through the door into the dim hallway. He could hear the children playing at the other end of the house and moved in that direction. The kitchen was a study of white tiles and salmon cupboards and bench tops. Jennifer was cutting sandwiches into triangles on a cutting board. She looked up, joy lighting her face.

"Dad!"

She rushed to him, threw her arms around his neck, and kissed his cheek. Then stepped back, glancing at Neil's sombre face. "It's so good to see you, Dad. I'm glad you decided to come over today, I was hoping you might."

"I brought vanilla slice and chocolate milk," he said, setting the bags on the bench.

She grinned. "My favourites."

"I know." He kissed her cheek. "It's good to see you sweetie."

His reunion with the children was far more exuberant. Five-year-old Sophie hugged his leg while three-year-old Daniel launched himself at Rob's neck. He sat on the couch, letting them clamber all over him. Both talking at the same time, telling him everything at once.

He laughed, listening and nodding, trying to keep up.

"Well, I gotta go—got some things to do. Sorry I can't stay, Rob. I'll see you soon, no doubt," interrupted Neil.

Rob watched him walk out in surprise. Neil didn't often leave him alone with his daughter and grandchildren. He'd barely spent a moment with them in the past five years, without Neil hovering nearby. He glanced at Jennifer with one eyebrow quirked, she shrugged in response.

After Neil left, it was as though all the tension in the room had gone with him. Jennifer's shoulders lowered and her smile returned. She took Rob and the kids out into the backyard with a plateful of sandwiches and the treats Rob had brought with him for dessert.

Together, they watched the children play. For a single moment, it felt like they were a normal, happy family. Joy bubbled in Rob's soul, along with a reaching sadness that tinged the moment with pain.

"I wish it could be like this all the time," murmured Jen, as though she could read Rob's thoughts.

He grunted. "It could be... if Neil would only..."

She interrupted him. "He does the best he can."

"Really?"

She faced him with resignation painted across her pretty features. Her blue eyes darkened, and her lips turned down at the corners. "Yes, really. He loves us. He doesn't always know how to show it, but he does."

Rob scoffed. Then he saw the pain it caused her and regretted it. He reached a hand to cup her shoulder, squeezed once. "I'm sorry, I'll try..."

"Thank you."

"I guess I don't understand why you married him, why you stay. He doesn't let you see your friends anymore, or me either. Not really. It's been months since I've seen any of you, I always have to come here. You never come to Brisbane."

She shook her head. "He doesn't like it." Then bit her lip. "I mean, he prefers us to be close by."

"He prefers you to be close by? That's how you justify it? He's keeping you a virtual prisoner in your own home."

"It's not like that," she objected, running a hand over her

face. "He doesn't like to be alone, without us. He likes to know where we are, he cares."

"If he really cared, he'd give you freedom." Rob shook his head. What was she thinking? Was she thinking at all? Didn't she know how she sounded when she talked this way? It made no sense at all.

Jen leaned her elbows on her thighs, staring at the play gym the kids were climbing on. Sophie was a pirate, defending her territory from the invading forces led by Daniel.

She sighed. "I want you to get along. I need you to get along. Do you think you can do that, Dad?"

A lump formed in his throat. In profile, she looked so much like her mother it hurt. He reached for her face, stroked her cheek, and tucked a strand of brown hair behind her ear. "I'll try."

She faced him, and her eyes were full of pain. "Will you?"

"Yes, I promise. I will try to get along with Neil."

"Thank you, Daddy. I couldn't lose..." She didn't finish her sentence, but he knew what she was about to say. She couldn't lose her father, the only family she had left.

It was like a punch to his gut. Her words were clear. If he didn't play along, be nice to Neil, act like they were all one big happy family, Neil would cut him out of their lives.

5

22ND DECEMBER 1996

CABARITA BEACH

When Liz opened her eyes the next morning, she couldn't believe how late it was. A plover called nearby, and the twitter of birds outside her window was like a melody played on the backdrop of the sighing ocean.

She hadn't slept so well in months, possibly years. Perhaps it was the sound of waves crashing against the shore, or the deliciously comfortable bed. She couldn't say what it was that'd prompted her to sleep until nine o'clock, but she liked it. It felt almost wasteful to sleep so late, something she'd been taught to avoid since she was a little girl. *Waste not, want not*, had been her mother's favourite slogan. And yet, here she was, wasting the day away in bed. Yet, what else should she be doing?

After a hot shower, she dressed in sensible clothing,

including her favourite blue blouse and a pair of denim three-quarter length jeans, not sure of what the day might bring, but hopeful that it would entail something other than reading in the sitting room. She headed downstairs, steeling herself against the rush of dread that came with facing the world alone, again.

She found a woman seated in the breakfast nook, along with several other guests who'd had a late start and were still sipping the remnants of their morning coffee.

"Good morning," said the woman. "I'm not sure we've met yet. I'm Mima, I'm the cook here at the Waratah Inn."

Liz reached out a hand to shake Mima's. Mima's grip was firm, her blue eyes twinkled above a set of half-moon spectacles perched on the end of her nose. Her greying hair curled wildly over her head. She pushed aside the newspaper she was reading.

"I'm Liz, it's a pleasure to meet you Mima."

"First time at the inn? Are you meeting someone?" asked Mima, she glanced behind Liz with a smile, then met Liz's gaze, eyebrows arched.

Liz nodded. "First time. And no, I'm here on my own." Her throat tightened at the words. She swallowed and continued. "It's beautiful. I'm looking forward to exploring."

"You'll have a wonderful time here. It's compulsory." Mima winked. "I hope you're hungry. The staff are still serving breakfast, and your server will be with you soon to take your order."

"Thank you." Liz slid into a chair closest to one of the large, rectangular windows, and peered out at the beautiful landscape of coastal gums, sea grass and squat bushes, intermingled with vivid wildflowers.

When she turned back, Mima was still looking at her, her brow furrowed. She offered a lopsided smile. "Liz, I hope you don't mind, and please don't feel as though you have to say yes, but I'm going with a friend to Tweed City, a shopping centre nearby, and I thought you might like to come with us."

Liz was taken aback. She hadn't expected the offer, and it came at her like a life preserver. "Really?"

Mima chuckled. "We're not doing anything exciting, just getting some groceries and supplies, but if you'd like to join us, you're more than welcome."

THE BUSTLE OF THE SHOPPING CENTRE WAS A PLEASANT contrast to the quiet, slow-paced meandering of the inn. The dress-code was casual, some people sporting swimsuits and bare feet, others in t-shirts, shorts, and sandals. Most looked as though they'd recently emerged from the surf, or from beneath the covers of their beds—fluffy, untamed hair, and glowing tans.

Liz studied the crowd passing by, her hands held in her lap, legs crossed at the ankles.

Mima set a plastic number on the table in front of her.

"Coffee's coming," she said with a smile.

Mima lowered herself into a chair beside Liz with a groan. "The old joints don't work as well as they used to.'

"You need to try water aerobics with me," added Betty, slumping into a seat next to her. Betty was Mima's friend, they'd picked her up on the way to Tweed Heads. She grinned at Liz. "It makes all the difference, that and fish oil."

Mima rolled her eyes. "You and that fish oil. One day I'm going to turn around and you'll have turned into a cod, all googly-eyed and slimy."

Liz grinned. The two of them hadn't stopped bickering and teasing since they left the Betty's house, but it was good-natured. It was obvious how much they cared for one another.

"So, you two live together?" she asked.

Mima's eyes widened. "Ohhh... that sounds a bit scandalous. What do you think, Betty?"

Betty laughed a big belly laugh that made her arms jiggle. "Ah... a bit of scandal would be nice these days. I wouldn't mind some excitement. But alas no, we live next door to each other. Though, we might as well live together, as much as she's forever coming through my front door."

Liz chuckled. "I could do with a scandal myself, these days."

Mima and Betty exchanged a glance. "As young as you are, I'm sure there's plenty of that in the days ahead."

Liz inhaled a slow breath, shook her head. "Nope. I highly doubt that. My days are pretty mundane, nothing much to look forward to. And I'm not as young as you think... forty-seven."

Mima quirked an eyebrow. "Forty-seven is young, my dear. Trust us on that one."

Betty nodded; her head tilted to one side. "I'd love to be forty-seven again. That was a good age. I wouldn't want to be twenty-one again, torturous!"

Mima moaned. "Definitely not. But forty-seven, I could do all over. Wouldn't mind it at all. No aches and pains, everything working as it should, and you've figured out most of the things life's thrown your way. Yep. Definitely a good age."

Liz scrubbed her face with both hands. They didn't understand. No one could. Most people had things figured out by now, but not her. She'd managed to ignore all the signs, working happily away with her head buried in the sand, then it'd all come crashing down around her ears before she'd had a chance to realise anything was the matter.

"Not for me."

Mima sighed. "Do you mind me asking...?"

Liz shook her head, feeling the twinge of a pain in her

throat. "No, it's fine. I don't mind. Two years ago, my husband left me for the architectural associate I hired to help me at our shared business."

Mima's nostrils flared and Betty's lips pressed together until fine lines pulled from her lips to her nose, puckering her mouth.

"They live together now. My daughter is in London, following her career—which is wonderful and I'm so proud of her, but I miss her. And my son left home at the start of the year to go to University in Melbourne." She choked back a sob. "He could've stayed in Sydney, but he wanted to go to Melbourne. Then, six months ago my husband decided we should dissolve the business partnership... you know, since we couldn't all keep working together under the circumstances. So now, I live all alone in an enormous house that we designed together when we were happy and in love, and that I've spent the past twenty years decorating in anticipation of all the parties, gatherings and family events..." She hesitated, the lump in her throat too large to ignore.

Mima reached out a large, wrinkled hand and rested it on Liz's arm. She squeezed gently. "That's a lot to cope with all at once."

Betty's dark grey bob shimmered under the florescent lights as she shook her head. "I'm sorry to hear that, Liz."

A waitress set three coffees on the table along with three slices of cheesecake.

Mima's brow furrowed. "We didn't order..."

"I bought them for us, thought it would be a nice treat. And a thank you for letting me tag along," interrupted Liz.

Mima's eyes widened. "Well, thank you Liz. That is very kind. I haven't eaten cheesecake in... well, it's been a while. The doctor has me on this strict diet. But I think I can manage one treat."

They fell silent a moment, each seemingly caught up in

their own thoughts. Why had she opened up to them that way? She was usually more reticent. She liked to keep up appearances, and hated people pitying her. But there was something about Mima and Betty that made her feel comfortable, like they wouldn't judge her no matter what she said. And being away from home, in a strange town, she didn't have to worry about the gossip following her home. Half the north shore had gabbed about her separation when it happened.

For six whole months their marriage was the subject of conversation at PTA meetings and at the golf club where she and Cam had been members for over a decade. It was nice to be anonymous, even if it was only for a week.

"You know, life will go on," murmured Mima around a bite of cheesecake.

Betty nodded her agreement.

"Do you think so?" Liz sipped her coffee, her eyes fixed on Mima. "Because sometimes it really doesn't feel like it will."

"It will, and not only that, you might well find the best is yet to come." Mima chuckled.

Liz huffed. "I highly doubt that."

"I know it's hard to imagine now, but things won't stay like this, not if you don't let them. You could stay mired in self-pity and grief, if that's what you choose to do. Or, you could grab life by the horns and decide that you're not going to let it knock you down that way. You could make it into something... whatever you want it to be."

"I don't know..." Liz couldn't imagine anything changing. It felt set, as though concrete had enveloped her life and would hold her in place there forever.

"Haven't you ever heard... life is what you make it?" asked Betty, licking cheesecake from her lips.

Liz dipped her head. "Yes, of course. It's what we tell teenagers to motivate them to do something…"

"It's more than that… it's true. And not just for teenagers. Your life isn't over. You've got plenty of years ahead of you. Now it's time for you to decide how you want your life to look and go after it."

"Maybe…"

Mima inhaled a deep breath. "I changed my life once."

"You did?" Liz leaned forward. She loved hearing other people's stories. Loved seeing how their lives had woven together in strands to make them who they were.

"Yes. I was headed down one path, and I turned it around, with the help of my best friend. I was in love, you know, and I lost him."

An ache passed through Liz's heart. "Oh, I'm sorry, Mima."

Mima offered a wan smile. "Thank you, my dear. Yes, completely and utterly in love. It was silly really, how quickly we fell for one another, but sometimes these things happen. Not often, but every now and then, people fall in love the moment they set eyes on one another, and that's what happened with us. He was killed in the war, I'm afraid, and that was that."

Liz's eyes watered. "Oh, that's horrible."

Betty nodded silently as she stirred a spoon around and around in her coffee.

"It was, just horrible. I didn't think I'd ever recover from that, let me tell you. And in the end, it took an act of the will. I had to decide how I wanted my life to look, and I had to make some changes. So, that's what I did. And you can do it too. You just have to accept your new reality first, and maybe do some forgiving, put the past behind you. Then, you'll be ready to move forward. There's so much life ahead of you, love."

Mima patted her arm.

Liz's throat tightened. Was there? Life ahead of her? She'd already given up, let go of the possibility that anything good would come her way now. It was hard to picture a future that included anything other than lonely days in her big, empty house.

She thought about Mima's words as they drove back to the inn. Her eyes were fixed on the whizzing landscape, and she felt an ache in the back of her throat that wouldn't go away. Why was she holding onto the past? As Mima said, she should let it go, move on. For some reason, she couldn't seem to do it. Didn't want to do it. It'd been her dream, the life she'd built for herself. That was the way she'd imagined her life all those years ago, and it was what she'd set out to achieve. She didn't want another life; she wanted that one. Letting go would mean admitting to herself that dream didn't exist any longer. That it never would.

And how could she forgive Cam for destroying that? He wasn't sorry, he didn't deserve her forgiveness.

Back in her room, she lay on the bed and stared up at the ceiling. White crown moulding. A single overhead light, a small chandelier, in the same style as the larger one that hung over the staircase. She couldn't get Mima and Betty's words out of her head. Was she giving up before she should? What could her life look like?

She reached for the telephone and dialled London. Danita picked up on the third ring. "Hello, this is Dani."

"Dani, sweetheart it's Mum."

"Oh hi, Mum. It's good to hear your voice."

"You too, my love. How are you?"

She could almost hear Dani's smile through the line, closing her eyes to picture her daughter's beautiful face. She missed seeing her, holding her, hearing about her day in person.

"I'm fine, working hard. Looking forward to Austria. We leave tomorrow, I think I have everything packed. Can't believe I'm spending Christmas on the slopes. It's so surreal."

Liz smiled. She hadn't thought about it that way before—her daughter was living her own dream. Her excitement about the adventure ahead was palpable.

"I'm so glad for you, honey. You're going to have a wonderful time. Just... you know, stay safe."

"Oh, Mum, you know I will. I'm always careful."

"I worry..."

Danita laughed softly. "I know you do, Mum. I promise to be extra careful just for you."

"Thank you." How had she missed that her daughter was a grown woman with a life of her own to live? She'd been so caught up in the fact that Danita had moved away, leaving a gap in her life, she hadn't thought about how much it meant to Danita to do it.

"When did you become such an amazing, strong, adventurous woman?" she asked, her voice catching in her throat.

"I learned from you, of course," replied Danita with a laugh.

Liz shook her head, covering her eyes with one hand. "Well, I miss you."

"Miss you too, Mum. I hope you have a wonderful Christmas. Don't know if I'll be able to call, probably not until I get back to London. Okay?"

Liz nodded. "Yes, of course. That's fine. Have a wonderful Christmas."

She hung up the phone, her hand still cupping her forehead. Danita's words hung in her thoughts. She'd learned from Liz. It wasn't how Liz saw herself—adventurous and strong. No, that was someone else. Still, maybe she'd been that way once. Since then she'd shrunk into a person she barely recognised anymore. Someone weak, small, and timid.

Someone afraid to face life, who stayed within the walls of her house, unwilling to step out into the world in case it hurt her more than it already had.

The phone jangled and made her jump. Her heart thudded and she reached for it. Dani must be calling her back, though she didn't remember giving her the inn's number.

"Hello, is this Liz?" A man's voice echoed down the line.

Liz's brow furrowed. "Yes, this is Elizabeth Cranwell."

"Oh, hi, Liz, it's Rob from next door. Wondering if you still want to take that walk along the beach?"

SEAGULLS CIRCLED ONE END OF THE BEACH. THE WIND WAS cool against her hot skin, drying the trails of sweat that'd formed on her temples. The burning sun dipped toward the horizon, still furious at the world. The sand was warm as Liz's toes dug into it. She pressed forward, glad of the exercise. It reminded her of her strength, of the life that flowed through her veins. She was alive. It wasn't over yet.

Beside her, Rob moved in unison, his eyes fixed on the horizon where azure water met blue sky. She glanced up, clouds hung still, as though caught in the humidity of the day, heavy and low.

"Beautiful day," offered Rob.

She smiled his way. "Yes, it is. I love the beach."

"Where are you from?" he asked.

"Dee Why," she replied.

"Is that close to the beach?"

She nodded. "Northern beaches. I can walk down to the shore if I want to. Though, I don't often want to in summer." She laughed. "My air-conditioned car is far more appealing."

He chuckled. "I understand that."

"And you?"

"I live in St. Lucia, in Brisbane."

"Oh, I haven't been there." She studied his profile. Strong, yet sensitive. He had a handsome nose, and the remnants of dimples in his cheeks when he smiled.

"It's a nice place to live. I'm a professor at the University of Queensland, so I live nearby and ride my bike to work. Lots of trees, rolling hills, cafes, restaurants, independent book shops. You know... university life."

She grinned. "Ah yes, I remember those days. I loved university. Of course, I thought I was so busy and tired. Then I got married, had children and realised I had no idea what tired was." She laughed.

He nodded. "That is so true. I have students tell me they weren't able to get an assignment done because they're too busy. I have to work hard not to laugh, but I guess they're really only a few years into adulthood and haven't worked out how to manage their time yet."

She grinned. "That's my son. He's in his first year of university. He's loving it, but I'm afraid he's focusing more on his social life than his studies."

"Pretty normal, I think. He'll figure it out before his final year."

"I hope so," she replied. It was hard to let go of being a mother after so many years in the role, but David was an adult now and responsible for his own life. At least, that's what she had to keep reminding herself whenever they spoke on the phone.

"What do you do for a living?" he asked.

He couldn't know how complicated it was. How much should she share? She wasn't working. Her husband had been her business partner for most of her professional life. And now she was unemployed. A beach bum. Well, not exactly. The life of a beach bum sounded far more appealing than what she really spent her time doing — which included trips to the gym, the shops and a lot of wandering around a stylish and very clean house.

"I'm an architect."

"Wow. I've always admired architects. You design things that get built and that shape communities, cities. Beautiful — I wish I was creative. Alas, I'm only a scientist." His eyes glowed, and met hers, sending an unexpected bolt of electricity down her spine. He was attractive in an unexpected way, she wondered about his story. At their age, everyone had a story. He didn't wear a ring and had asked her to take a walk with him, most likely he was single.

"Yes, it is pretty special. I've always loved what I do. It feels like a privilege."

"Do you work for yourself?" he asked, as they stepped out of the shifting dry sand and onto the wet sand.

"Actually, I'm taking a break." It was true, and it was all she wanted to share at this stage. As Ivy often said, there was no need to go bleeding all over people. Besides, she'd sound desperate and pathetic. She didn't want him to see her that way.

"Sometimes we all need a break," was all he said in reply.

She nodded.

They walked until it was dark. They talked about their lives, and Liz was so taken up in what Rob was saying she didn't notice when the sun sank and threw the beach into darkness. Crickets chirruped while Rob shared about his work, his love of cycling and the outdoors. Shadows deepened as she talked about her family, her friends and the dreams she'd had as a child. The steady rhythm of the waves soothed her soul, the vastness of the ocean comforted her. The man beside her resonated with strength and confidence that drew her in. Their conversation flowed, comfortable and with ease. And for a time, she forgot that her life was in ruins.

6

CABARITA BEACH

The morning sun glowed bright in the sky. It was already well above the horizon and had heated the day until it was almost unbearable, even though he'd only eaten breakfast a half hour earlier. Rob picked up the pace, eager to make it back to the inn before he was incinerated. He hadn't thought to wear sunscreen at that time of morning, and he was already regretting the oversight.

The walk was his way of clearing his head. He was meeting Jen, Neil, and the kids at Point Danger for a picnic later and wanted to prepare himself. He had to get along with Neil, that's what Jen had asked of him, so surely, he could manage it. He'd bite his tongue, nod, smile. It wouldn't be so hard. Surely. Still, he wished he had someone to go with him, someone to distract him away from the fact that he'd like to grab Jen and the kids and make a run for it. He grimaced. This was going to be a disaster.

Dark rocks marked the end of the cove and dotted the beach here and there. The tide was low, exposing more of them, and seagulls hovered, swooping down, then up again as they caught their breakfast in shallow rock pools.

A woman sat, perched on one of the smaller rocks, her legs folded to her body. She stared out at the waves, the morning breeze moving her blonde hair. It was Liz.

Their walk together the previous evening had left him intrigued. She was an interesting woman, someone he felt he'd like to get to know better. Though he knew there wasn't much point, since she lived in Sydney, more than twelve hours drive from his home.

Still, he couldn't ignore the pull. She was intelligent, mysterious, attractive... something about her made him want to know more. She was keeping something to herself, something she was mulling over, grieving perhaps. There was a sadness about her that tugged at his heart.

"Good morning," he said.

She startled. She must have been lost in her thoughts and hadn't heard his approach.

"Oh, good morning, Rob. Lovely day for a walk."

He nodded. "Beautiful, although I'm anxious to get out of this sun. I can feel it burning the back of my neck, every step I take." He laughed awkwardly. Small talk wasn't his strength.

"What do you have planned for the day?" she asked, standing, and brushing the sand from her shorts.

"I'm meeting my daughter and her family for a picnic lunch at the beach. How about you?"

"Oh, that sounds lovely. I don't know... I haven't decided what to do yet. I thought I might catch the bus up to the shops and watch a movie...still pondering." She grinned, but the sadness was still there.

He hesitated. Should he invite her? It might help him get through the lunch, maybe even prompt Neil to be more civil.

"I have an idea, why don't you come with me? It's low-key; a simple family picnic. I know Jen wouldn't mind, and I'd love to have you join us."

Her brows knitted together over blue eyes. "Oh no, I wouldn't want to intrude on your family day."

"Nonsense," he replied. "It's absolutely fine. Please, it would be a pleasure to have you come and join us."

She hesitated, glanced over her shoulder toward the inn, then back again, meeting his gaze. "Are you sure? I really don't want to be a pain. Honestly, I'm perfectly fine occupying myself."

"I enjoy your company," he replied, "and it would give us a chance to spend more time together, plus you'll really be doing me a favour since I'm not a big fan of my son-in-law, and you can help distract me from my desire to throttle him."

She laughed at that, her eyes sparkling. "Okay then, you've convinced me."

❧

THEY DROVE TOGETHER, THEIR CONVERSATION FLOWING AS though they'd known each other for years. Rob was pleasantly surprised at how natural it was for him to talk to her and found himself cracking jokes and making her laugh in a way he hadn't done in years. He surprised himself with his own charm, a skill he'd thought long lost. He was completely taken by her grace, something that seemed to come easily to her; effortless, like the simple beauty of her face, or the way her hair fell across her cheeks.

By the time they arrived, he was convinced he'd made the right choice by inviting her. She'd definitely give him the distraction he needed to avoid conflict with Neil, and it mean more time with her too, which was something he was rapidly realising would come to an end sooner than he'd like it to. It was as though a stopwatch hung over his head, counting down the time until his holiday was over.

He pulled the car into the Point Danger parking lot and was happy to see one space open. By the time they climbed from the car he'd spotted Jen and Neil. They'd claimed one of the picnic tables and Jen had set up a red tablecloth held in place by a picnic basket. Rob had stopped along the way to grab a few supplies as well and pulled the bag from the car boot before leading Liz over to meet his family.

Jen greeted him with a hug. "Hi Dad."

"Jen, Neil, this is Liz, a friend from the inn where I'm staying."

Neil didn't respond. Jen arched an eyebrow momentarily, a smile tugging at the corner of her mouth. "Oh? How nice to meet you, Liz."

Liz's cheeks were tinged with pink. She shook Jen's outstretched hand. "Lovely to meet you, Jen and Neil. I hope you don't mind me crashing your party."

"Not at all, not at all. We're glad to have you," replied Jen, taking Liz by the arm, and leading her toward the lookout where Rob could see the kids playing.

"How's it going, Neil?" asked Rob. He'd play his part, do his best to get along. Then, he'd spend the rest of the day with Liz, Jen, and the kids.

Neil grunted. Crossed his arms over his chest and gave Rob the side-eye. "I guess you feel free to invite whoever you want to our family picnic, huh?"

Rob's eyes narrowed. "I guess I do."

"Figures."

"Is that okay with you, Neil?"

"Nope. But don't listen to me, do what you like."

Rob shook his head. "Okay, fine. I will."

Neil huffed.

"Nice to see you again, Neil." Rob strode toward the look-out, his blood boiling. How anyone could get along with a man like that was beyond him. The best thing he could do would be to keep his distance for the rest of the picnic.

The kids rushed him as soon as they saw him. They immediately took up all of his attention, wanting him to look through the large binoculars that were positioned around the lookout's railings.

"Will we see a whale, Grandpa?" asked Sophie, as he held her up to look through the eyepiece.

He chuckled. "Not likely, sweetheart. Not this time of year. More likely you'll see a pod of dolphins if you look hard."

Sophie squinted for a while, but then gave up, heading up the grassy hill to play with her brother.

Jen looped her arm through his as they walked along the footpath. Cliffs dropped off beyond the railing, plummeting toward crashing waves that broke themselves against their rocky, jagged faces sending sea spray high and white into the air. In the distance a tiny yacht sailed, leaning into the wind.

"He doesn't like strangers," said Jen, as if in apology.

"He doesn't like anyone," replied Rob.

Jen shook her head. "You knew it would cause tension. Don't get me wrong, I'm glad you invited her, she's wonderful."

They both looked at where Liz was wrestling with the children in the grass. Squeals of delight echoed back to them on the wind.

Jen laughed. "She's great. It's not about that; you knew bringing a stranger to our picnic would make him angry."

"I don't much care what makes Neil angry," replied Rob.

"You should," she replied, her smile fading.

Rob's heart fell. Of course, he hadn't thought it through.

Who would suffer the consequences of Neil's anger but his daughter and grandchildren? His stomach churned.

"You can leave him, you know?"

She faced him her eyes full of pain. "No, I can't."

"Yes, you can."

Neil's shout broke through their conversation. Rob turned his attention to where Neil stood, beckoning them all over. They walked back to the picnic table. The kids were already seated in front of a paper-wrapped package.

"Fish and chips will get cold if we don't eat soon," grunted Neil.

They sat, Jen unwrapped the package and tore off small pieces for each person to use as a plate. Then, they each reached for a steaming piece of fish and a few chips and filled up their makeshift plates with the bounty.

The kids ate, chattering happily with Liz, who seemed to be their new best friend. Rob watched on, smiling, as he and Jen discussed his work, how much his students had changed over the years and what he planned on doing with his back-yard. She was trying to convince him to build a pool, he objected that he wouldn't use it.

"But we'll use it," she replied with a chuckle. "The kids would love to have a pool to play in when we come up."

"Yeah, all those times you visit," retorted Rob.

He didn't realise how the words would sound until they were out of his mouth. Jen fell silent and glanced Neil's way.

Rob's smile faded. "Sorry, I didn't mean it like that. Only joking around."

"It's fine," replied Jen.

Neil glowered. "I can afford to build us a pool if I want to. I don't think we need one, that's all."

"Of course, I didn't mean..." Jen's voice faded, she stared at the cooling piece of fish in front of her, eyes wide.

"Is Sophie still enjoying school?" asked Rob.

Jen offered him a half smile; her eyes full of gratitude. "Yes, she loves it. Mrs. Brown, her teacher, says she's confident, happy, and loves reading."

He tousled Sophie's hair. "That's my girl."

"It's fun, and I get to play with my friends every day," added Sophie, a grin splitting her face in two.

"I wanna go to school too," added Daniel with a pout, his brown eyes wide.

"Won't be long," said Liz in a cheery voice, "You'll be at school before you know it."

"I always loved school," added Rob. "I think the two of you are going to love it as well. It's fun to learn new things and make new friends."

Sophie nodded with enthusiasm. Daniel listened as he chewed.

Rob inhaled a slow breath. Time to try again. He didn't want to exclude Neil from the conversation, it would end with him blaming Jen for purposely leaving him out. It'd happened before, he didn't want it to be the way things ended today.

"So, Neil, how's work going for you?"

Neil's eyes narrowed as he chewed on a chip. "Fine."

"Still working for that company... what was the name?" Rob waited with a smile pressed to his lips.

Neil glowered, then faced Jen, still chewing. "Did you tell him? I said not to tell him. You love humiliating me, don't you?"

Jen's eyes grew wide, her mouth dropped open. "No, I didn't say anything... I didn't..."

"She didn't tell me anything. I have no idea what you're talking about, Neil. I was only making small talk." Irritation burned in Rob's gut. What was wrong with the man? It was a simple question, social chit-chat.

"Nothing more than small talk. Right. Only, I know this

one, and she's gabbed to you all about my business, I can tell that sure enough." He stood to his feet, towering over Jen, his face thunderous. "I asked you to do this one thing, keep it to yourself. My idiot boss didn't know what was best for him, disrespecting me like that, and now you're disrespecting me in the same way. It's time you learned how to show your husband some respect. Get up, we're leaving."

"What? No. We're not finished..." Jen's objection hung in the air.

Neil grabbed her by the arm, eliciting a cry from her lips.

The children stopped eating. Daniel's eyes glimmered with tears. Sophie stared at the food, unmoving.

"Come on kids, get in the car," demanded Neil, striding toward the parking lot.

Jen bit down on her lip, nodding goodbye to Rob who stood beside the picnic table, hands balled into fists by his sides, and hurried after her husband. Rob knew if he tried to intervene it would only make things worse for Jen. He'd done that before as well and learned from his mistakes. If only she'd leave him. But she wouldn't, so everything he did had consequences for her and the kids. He had to keep out of it. He hadn't meant to cause friction. He should've kept his mouth shut.

The children hurried after their parents. Sophie spun around to wave goodbye. Rob raised a hand, his breath coming in hurried gasps as he fought the urge to run after them.

As the car sped out of the lot, Liz moved to stand beside him, one hand pressed to her mouth. They stood that way, in silence, for several long minutes.

"I'm sorry about that," he said, around a lump in his throat. He coughed to clear it, then continued. "Sorry I brought you into it."

She shook her head, took his hand in hers and met his gaze. "No, don't be sorry. It's not your fault."

His throat constricted. "I didn't mean..."

"You did nothing wrong. You were making conversation. He was the one who turned it into something else."

"I should've known." He shook his head, frustration at his own naiveté building in his gut.

"No one could've known. He's a time bomb waiting to go off."

He nodded. "Yes, he is."

"I can see why you're not a fan," she said in a droll tone.

He laughed. "Yeah."

She linked her fingers through his. "Come on, let's throw this food away and find some ice cream. I could do with something sweet after that."

Tears pricked his eyes and he blinked them away. The warmth of her hand in his comforted him. Having her by his side gave him strength.

He nodded. "Good idea."

7

The inn was quiet as the heat of the afternoon shimmered outside her bedroom window. She'd seen a few guests in the sitting room enjoying the air-conditioning, but most seemed to either be out, or hidden away in their rooms, riding out the heat wave. Elizabeth stood by the window; her arms crossed over her chest. A few puffy grey clouds promised rain but kept their distance as if afraid to come too close to the scorched coast.

The lunch with Rob's family had shaken Liz more than she cared to admit. He hadn't warned her, other than a few words about not caring to spend much time with his son-in-law. Though how does a person explain something like that to someone they've only recently met? She couldn't blame him for not talking about it. On the ride home, he'd said he hoped she'd be something of a buffer and would keep him distracted from causing tension, he wouldn't have taken her if he'd thought it would fall apart the way it did. He apologised and she told him it wasn't his fault, no one could've known, or done anything differently.

It puzzled her to realise he blamed himself somehow for the way the picnic ended.

Seeing Rob's family had reminded her of how much she missed her own. Before it'd all fallen apart, she'd had a lovely time with the children. They were cute, sweet, and full of life. She'd remembered how much she enjoyed being a mother, playing with her own children, listening to their squeals of delight and trills of laughter.

What was she doing with her life?

She'd let Cam bring it crashing down around her ears, as though she had no control over it. Over anything.

What did she want? Where would she go now?

She still loved architecture. Maybe she should call a few of her old clients when she got back to town, see if they still wanted to work with her. A few had called after the business closure, but she hadn't been in the right state of mind. She'd told them she was out of the business and hung up with a heavy heart. But she'd known many of them for years. They were friends, if nothing else. They'd give her a second chance; she was sure of it.

She could set up her own business in the home office. She'd worked there many a time in the past, while the children played in the background. She could do it again, even if the house was hollow and empty, and silence filled the halls. Maybe she'd turn on the radio.

Her own thoughts were tiring. She'd always been so confident, independent, and sure of herself and where she was headed. These days, her inner monologue was whiny, insecure, and uncertain. For the first time in two years, she wanted to switch it off. To stop listing all the reasons why her life was unfair, why nothing good could be salvaged from the wreckage that lay around her. Irritation at herself twisted a knot in her stomach.

She walked to the bed, lay on her back, and reached for the telephone on the bedside table.

Margot answered after the first few rings. "Hubbard residence, this is Margo Hubbard," she said in a clipped voice.

"It's Liz."

"Oh hi, Liz, how are you?"

"I'm fine. I wasn't expecting you to answer the phone, since you're at Frank's brother's house. Are you sitting by it, hoping it will ring?" Liz chuckled.

Margot sighed. "You tease, but you're not completely wrong. Frank is playing twenty-one with his brother, things always get a bit overwrought when they do that. They're both highly competitive. Anyway, I ordered us all some pizza and haven't moved from my seat by the phone since. I thought, maybe if I sit here for a few minutes, nobody will notice I'm missing, and I can have some peace and quiet. And then you called! I'm so glad you called, honey. It's the best Christmas gift ever, to hear your voice right now."

Liz squeezed the bridge of her nose with her fingertips. "You too. Seriously, I feel like I'm going to cry. I miss you so much, and it's only been a few days."

"Are things that bad?" asked Margot, concern edging her voice.

"No, no... really it's actually not as bad as I thought it'd be. But, it's still hard... I feel very alone." She laughed, but the sound caught in her throat.

"You know, Ivy and I could come up there, join you for a day or two before you head back..."

"Really? I mean, you don't have to do that. I'll be okay. I don't want to put you out."

"Sure... Frank and I are flying to Sydney the day after Christmas. I could grab Ivy and head your way, so we could all have a day at the inn together... what do you think? Would that help you feel better? It wouldn't be only for your benefit. I know I could do with a day of relaxation after this."

Liz smiled. "Yes, yes, yes! That would be amazing. I'd love you to come up here. It's so beautiful, I think you'd have a great time."

"Fine, it's settled. Give me the number for reception and I'll book us in."

They talked over the details for a few more minutes. Liz found herself anticipating their visit more with each moment that passed. She'd be able to show them around, take them for a walk in the cove, visit Tweed Heads. In the end, Margot decided they could stay for three days, meaning Liz would only have to spend one more day alone after they returned to Sydney. She could barely contain her relief and excitement.

"I can't wait for you both to get here. It's going to be so much fun!" she fairly squealed into the phone.

Margot laughed. "I'm looking forward to it as well. After spending time with Frank's family, I'm going to need to unwind before I go back to work, or I may not make it."

By the time she'd hung up the phone, Liz's demeanour was completely changed. She straightened, swung her legs over the bed and wriggled her toes, a smile lighting up her face. Things were looking better and better all the time. Even her time so far at the inn had been much better than she'd imagined it would be. Rob's friendship, their walks, conversations... she hadn't laughed so much with a man in as long as she could remember. Time with him made her spirit feel light, happy, carefree. She was almost the woman she'd been before she had children.

She wasn't sure why she hadn't mentioned him to Margot, only that she wanted to keep him to herself for now. As much as she loved her friend, she knew any mention of a man would make Margot's ears prick up and have her imagination running wild. She'd never understand that what they shared was friendship, nothing more. It couldn't be more, they both lived in different cities, and besides, she was certain he didn't see her in a romantic light. He was simply being kind, thoughtful, caring. She'd held his hand while they walked to the ice cream shop earlier, and it'd been comfortable, easy. The attraction was there, at least on her end, but she was mature enough to allow it, without believing it impossible to ignore.

Feelings could be ignored. She ignored her own all the time. Every time she wanted to smack Cam in the face, she ignored the urge. Every time she wanted to scream in a public place, she resisted. Whenever she felt like crawling into a dark hole and hiding, she pushed that aside and, instead, finished doing whatever it was she was supposed to do, with a faux smile pressed firmly to her face. It was what adults did, they pushed through their feelings to do what was right.

And right now, Rob needed her friendship and care. She could see he was struggling with what was happening in his family, and he'd asked her to tag along earlier because he needed her help and wanted someone to be there for him.

He hadn't talked to her yet about what'd happened to his wife, but she'd guessed his wife must have passed since he didn't talk about an ex. If he wanted to open up to her about it, he would in his own time. Though of course, they only had a few days together. They'd realised during the course of one conversation they were both booked into the Waratah Inn until the day before New Year's Eve. A funny, if meaningless, coincidence. It'd given her comfort at the time, before her conversation with Margot. Now she'd have other friends to share her holiday with, as well as Rob.

Her energy flagged. Either she'd have to take a nap or drink a coffee. One or the other. She decided on coffee, since the phone call had invigorated her and inspired her to do something. She wasn't sure what she should do, but she wanted to get out and enjoy the rest of her day. It was a shame the way the picnic had ended so abruptly, though she'd enjoyed their ice cream together afterward. Maybe she should see if Rob wanted to join her for the afternoon.

She knocked on his door, but he didn't answer. Perhaps he'd already gone out again, or maybe he'd headed to the cove for a walk to clear his thoughts.

Downstairs, she found Bindi checking people in at the reception desk. She stood in line to wait her turn.

"Good afternoon, Mrs. Cranwell. How is your stay so far?" asked Bindi, a bright smile lighting up her pretty face.

Liz nodded. "It's lovely. Thank you. I was wondering if you have any afternoon activities I could do... I feel like going out, but I'm not really sure where to go."

Bindi laughed. "Of course, let's see..." She reached for some brochures and spread them in front of Liz. "You could go horse riding on the beach, or there's probably a movie on at the cinema. We also have a few people headed up to wander around Surfer's Paradise if you care to join them. And here's a sunset river cruise—they serve tea on board the boat."

Liz studied the images of a boat with laughing couples seated at lavishly set tables for two. Her eyes narrowed. "The river cruise looks perfect."

Or at least it would be if she had someone to go with. She glanced around the inn. Where was Rob?

"Wonderful, I'll give them a call and book you in." Bindi reached for the telephone.

"Just a minute. You haven't seen Rob around, have you?"

"Mr. Patch?" asked Bindi.

"Yes."

"I think I saw him go into the sitting room a few minutes ago."

"Thank you!" called Liz, as she headed in that direction.

She found him reading a book, one leg crossed over the other, glasses balanced on the end of his nose.

He glanced up at her with a smile. "Hi, Liz."

She slid into a chair beside him. "Hi. Are you busy this afternoon?"

❧✤❧

COOL AIR DRIFTED OFF THE RIVER'S SURFACE AND enveloped Liz in a pleasant respite from the day's stifling heat. She smiled at Rob who leaned on the balcony railing beside her, his eyes fixed on hers. He grinned in reply.

"This is nice."

"Hmmm... Very nice. Thanks for coming with me."

He nodded. "Happy to do it. Actually, I'm glad you thought to invite me, I needed to get my mind off what happened today. I'd planned on spending the entire day with the family, so I was at a bit of a loose end."

The Tweed River stretched out ahead of the boat as it chugged quietly toward the setting sun. A wide, dark shimmering expanse of water, sunlight glancing off its surface in dancing shadows with pale orange hints.

In the sky, pink fingers shot through with dashes of dark orange and bright yellow reached overhead, fading into deep blue as night drew in behind the boat. A mountain range traced a dark outline on the horizon, and the boat chugged toward it.

The tension that'd been lodged in Liz's shoulders left with a single exhale. Something about the beauty of nature always brought her a sense of peace.

Beside her, Rob leaned his arms on the railing and stared toward the setting sun. The warmth of its light gave his face a youthful look, took away the stress that stretched his skin taut around the mouth, and danced in his eyes as sparkles.

He faced her, a smile tugging at the corners of his mouth. "You look beautiful tonight," he said.

Her breath caught in her throat. "Thank you." She hadn't expected that. He was being kind, she'd barely had a chance to put on any makeup before the taxi had arrived to take them to the cruise, since they'd booked it so last minute.

"Do you mind if I ask you a personal question?" she said.

He shrugged. "Go ahead."

"You haven't spoken about your wife..."

He inhaled a sharp breath. "I haven't? Ah... well, that's good."

She arched an eyebrow. "Sorry?"

He laughed. "That didn't come out right. See, usually I talk too much about her, so the fact that I haven't brought her up yet is a good thing. At least, I think it is."

"Ah... okay." Liz scratched her head.

"She died. Cancer."

"I'm sorry."

"Thank you," he replied. "It was a long time ago, ten years actually. So, I've had plenty of time to get used to the situation. It took me most of that time, I'm afraid."

"I understand. That would've been very difficult."

His lips pulled into a tight line. "Yes, it was. I honestly don't know how I came out of it in the end. I think it was only because of Jen. I realised she needed me. She got engaged to Neil and I could see, even then, how bad the match was. I didn't know him as well as I do now, but it was clear from the beginning they weren't suited. So, I pulled myself out of my grief to try and help her. But it was too late, she went ahead with it anyway."

He sighed and ran fingers through his blonde curls, standing them on end. The few grey streaks around his temples shone silver in the fading, orange light.

"I'm sorry," was all she could think to say.

"Thanks."

They stood side by side, watching the sun sink beyond the mountains and the river fall dark. Rob moved closer so his shoulder touched hers, the slight pressure of his body against hers sent a shiver of goose bumps down her arm.

She leaned into him, resting her head on his shoulder.

❧ 8 ☙

24TH DECEMBER 1996

CABARITA BEACH

The buttons on Rob's shirt refused to cooperate. He focused his attention on getting them through the holes, while he stared at his reflection in the mirror. He'd decided on a blue striped button-down shirt, though it was probably more than was strictly necessary for a beachside town. Still, it was Christmas Eve and he was determined that the day with family would go better this time than it had the last.

He was going over to Jen and Neil's house, and intended to take a bunch of flowers as a peace offering. He'd stop by the shops on the way there and buy a few drinks as well. Whatever he could do to help calm the waters. Not that he thought it would help, but he was desperate to spend time with Jen and the kids, and he'd do whatever was needed to make that happen.

Finally done with buttons, he pressed his hands to his hips. Long pants on a day like today would probably be overdoing it. Perhaps he should change into shorts after all. It was fine inside, with the cool air, but as soon as he stepped outside into the furnace... he sighed. Sometimes it all felt too hard. Surely Jen could see what her life was becoming. Here he was, worrying over what to wear, so he didn't upset her husband and could spend time with his grandchildren. The ridiculousness of the situation almost made him laugh, but for the pain in his throat.

He strode to the phone and dialled her number. Since he hadn't spoken to her after the picnic, hoping to give Neil space to calm down, he felt he should call to make sure plans hadn't changed.

"Good morning, Jen," he said, in answer to the sound of her voice.

"Oh hi, Dad." She sounded low. He knew his daughter well enough to sense that, after only a few exchanged words.

"You okay this morning, sweetheart?"

She hesitated. "I'm fine."

"Are we still on for today? I thought I might drop by the shops on the way there if you need me to grab anything..."

Another pause. "Oh, right... Um... look, Dad, I don't think we can manage today."

"What?" His temper flared. What was Neil up to now? It was Christmas Eve for heaven's sakes.

"We're... we're busy today. Sorry, Dad. I should've called... I've been so... busy. I'm sure you can understand that."

His eyes narrowed and he slumped onto the bed. "Sweetheart, you've got to be honest with me. What's going on? Are you okay?"

"I'm fine, Dad." Her thin voice echoed down the line, unconvincing.

"Well, I don't know what to say then, Jen. I've come down

here to see you and the kids for Christmas. It's now Christmas Eve, and you're telling me not to come over. What should I think?"

A sound like a sob pierced his heart. "I'm sorry, Dad." Her voice was muffled, broken.

His heart broke with it. "No, I'm sorry. Forget I said anything. Only, I worry about you, my love. It doesn't sound like things are fine, I want to see you."

"I can't..."

Rob's face tightened, and he balled his free hand into a fist. "Something has to change, Jen."

"Tomorrow, Dad. We'll see you tomorrow. Okay?"

"Fine. Tomorrow."

He hung up the phone, stood and paced across the length of the room, both hands curled in fists now. It was an impossible situation. He was powerless to do anything to help her. He wanted to see his daughter and his grandchildren on Christmas Eve. Was that so much to ask? What were they doing that kept them so busy? He knew that was an excuse, but why did they need one?

What was going on over there?

He hated not knowing, hated not being able to do anything. That Jen had gotten herself into the situation no longer mattered, what he wanted more than anything was to help her get out of it. But how? She wouldn't listen to him, always stood up for Neil, said he was tired, stressed, overworked, frustrated, or misunderstood. It was always someone else's fault, never Neil's. And what about the kids? Just recalling the looks on their faces when Neil had shouted at Jen, strode to the car, made his heart ache and anger boil in his gut.

How could he help his daughter when she wouldn't let him?

He had to do something.

Rob burst through the door, slamming it shut behind him as he ran down the stairs. When he reached the front door, he had second thoughts. If he rushed over there now, it might only make things worse. What would he say? What excuse could he give for showing up, right after Jen had asked him not to? He hesitated, then backtracked through the living room. He reached the windows, peered out into the bright morning, then spun on his heel and headed for the door again.

He couldn't stay away and do nothing. It was obvious Jen was upset, but she wouldn't tell him what the matter was. He should go over there and teach Neil a thing or two about how to treat women, how to respect a father-in-law.

When he reached the door, his doubts stopped him again and he turned, this time more slowly, back into the living room.

If he did that, there'd be no going back. He'd likely be cut off from ever seeing his daughter and grandchildren again. Jen wasn't likely to change her mind and leave her husband. He couldn't risk it.

Still, if he didn't do something. Who would?

He aimed again for the front door; this time full of resolve. Before he got there, Mima stepped in front of him with a smile. Her grey curls bobbed, and her eyes sparkled. She wore a white apron around her ample waist and held a wooden spoon high in the air.

"Good morning, Rob. How are you on this fine day? Christmas Eve already, huh? Didn't that sneak up on us?"

He stopped mid-stride, eyes widening. "Oh, uh, good morning, Mima. It is, yes... funny how fast Christmas comes around each year."

Her eyes narrowed and her smile widened. "I can see that you're a man full of energy and vigour this morning." Mima looped her arm through Rob's and began to tug him in the direction of the kitchen. "So, I thought to myself, what would help a man expend some of that energy in a positive way? And guess what came to mind."

Rob stared at her blankly, even as she pulled him stumbling through the inn, her grasp on his arm firm and strong. "Uh... I don't know."

"Horse riding," she replied with a wink. "That's the ticket. A horse beneath you, the open trail ahead of you... perfect. Now, it just so happens that Jack is readying a group of would-be riders at this very moment. So, you're in luck!"

Rob pulled back. "Ah... no, thanks Mima. I don't think I'm up for horse riding right now..."

"Nonsense," she patted his arm and tugged him onward. "It's exactly what a young man like you needs in his life. Trust me, it's not the kind of thing you can do forever. You've got to take life by the horns, or reins in this case, while you can." She laughed. "Come on, we'd better get moving or you'll miss out entirely."

Rob surrendered and let himself be ushered through the back door and down the winding garden path to where a group of guests milled about a horse yard. Horses stood, dotted around the yard, already saddled. Guests patted long, sleek necks and murmured amongst themselves. Mima led Rob directly to Jack's side. Jack, sporting an Akubra hat, held a clipboard in his hands and was scanning the contents of a piece of paper tacked to it. He glanced up when they arrived.

"Morning, Mima," he said.

"Good morning, Jack, my love. I have someone here, in desperate need of a horse to ride. This is Rob, he'll be joining you this morning."

Jack quirked an eyebrow. "Oh? Hi, Rob, glad you could join us."

"Actually, I'm not really the horse-riding type..."

"That's horseman, Rob," replied Jack. "Put your foot here."

Jack held a stirrup toward Rob. Rob eyed it. He'd never ridden a horse in his life. He wasn't entirely certain that fifty-two was the right age to start. He lifted his foot, pushed it into the stirrup.

"Okay, great. Now up you go." Jack pushed and Rob heaved and found himself seated on the back of a brown horse with a black mane and tail, staring down at the ground. The saddle was a lot further from the ground than he'd thought it would be.

"Great. We'll head out in a few minutes. As soon as everyone's mounted up." Jack patted the horse on the neck with a wry smile, winked at Mima, then walked off.

Mima chuckled. "Have fun, Rob." Then she too was gone.

Rob's eyes narrowed. He felt a little as though he'd had no say in the matter. He could try climbing down, he supposed. Though what would he do, where would he go? He sighed and gathered up the reins. Maybe riding a horse along the beach wouldn't be so bad.

"Rob?" Liz's voice turned his head.

She was seated on a golden horse nearby. She urged the animal closer to his, a smile lighting up her face. "I didn't know you were coming."

He laughed. "Neither did I."

Confusion flitted over her pretty features. "Well, let's ride together. It's a beautiful morning for it."

She seemed almost a different woman to the one he'd met that first day. Her face was full of life and vibrance. She'd seemed sad when they'd exchanged room keys, defeated. Not today. Today she fairly glowed. He hoped he'd had something to do with the change, though he supposed it wasn't likely. She saw him as a friend, someone to pass the time with, no matter how much he was beginning to think of her as something more.

"Okay, but I have to warn you, I've never done this before."

"Don't worry, I'll help you. I've ridden plenty of times."

Just then, his horse began to walk. He startled. "Uh... what do I do?"

"Hold on," laughed Liz behind him.

He grabbed a hold of some mane along with the reins and held tight. The horse ambled over to a patch of grass, tugged the reins from his grasp with a jerk of its head and then bent to pluck at the grass.

"I think we're having a meal break," he called back to Liz.

"You have to show the animal you're in charge. Otherwise she'll completely take advantage of you."

He chuckled. "Ah... that's what I've been doing wrong. It explains a lot about my life."

Liz laughed. "Glad to help you sort out the real issues."

Finally, they got his horse to stop eating long enough to follow the rest of the group down to the beach. The animal fell into line behind Liz's golden horse, walking, trotting, clambering along a narrow, beaten trail until they were on the sand. Then the group fanned out. Some cantered, some horses wandered along the water's edge, others hung back, enjoying a leisurely stroll. Jack rode a black horse in the middle of it all, offering advice here, a word of encouragement there. He didn't speak much, but when he did, people listened. Rob wished he had the kind of confidence and ease with life Jack seemed to possess. He was a manly man, exuding strength and peace all at the same time.

"I think you're getting the hang of it now," said Liz, riding up beside him at a trot.

"Yeah, it's not so bad," he replied, with a shrug. "The view's all right too." He grinned.

She nodded. "It's truly beautiful here."

Waves curled toward the shore, white bubbles frothed as they hissed, then hurried back toward the ocean. The air was fresh and smelled of salt, and the sun beat down on their heads already, warming the helmet Jack had handed him to wear before they left.

"Beauty is truth, truth beauty, —that is all ye know on earth, and all ye need to know," murmured Liz.

He glanced at her in surprise. Keats', *Ode to a Grecian Urn*, was his favourite poem. "You like that verse?"

"Love it," she replied, a dreamy look in her eyes.

He mulled over her words in silence, watching as she trotted her horse toward the water. What were the chances she'd love the same poem as him? Would quote it to him while horse riding together on the beach? He wasn't much of a romantic, but even he could see the romance in the moment. Was there a chance she'd see it too? Or perhaps he was only imagining it because he longed for it. The strangeness of that longing surprised him. He hadn't thought about romance in years, hadn't felt desire in as long.

He pushed his horse after her using his heels, the way Jack had shown them how to do earlier at the stables. It worked, the horse responded and set off at a trot. When he reached Liz, he tugged on the reins and the animal slowed.

"Have you decided what you're doing tomorrow?" he asked.

She shook her head, colour invading her cheeks. "I suppose I'll be here. Have a quiet day at the inn. I've booked lunch at a hotel. Then, maybe I'll read a book."

"That sounds nice..." He wasn't sure what to say.

She offered him a half smile. "You're right. It will be lovely. Quiet but relaxing."

"Can I ask—do you have family?"

"Yes. My daughter is in London, my son Tasmania. He decided to spend the holidays with his girlfriend's family."

Rob nodded. "Ah... I see."

"It's fine, of course. He's a grown man now, so I have to expect that he'll have a life of his own. Still, it's my first year... without all of them. I'm not quite used to it yet."

He could see she was struggling to find the words, that it hurt more than she was letting on. She was trying to be strong.

"I understand." And he did. He'd felt the same for almost a decade. Ever since his wife died, and his daughter married a man who did everything he could to keep Rob at arm's length.

"And my husband... sorry ex-husband... is having Christmas with his new girlfriend and her family. She also happens to be my former employee, and because of that he folded our shared business after decades together, since it made her uncomfortable for us to continue working together." Her eyes flashed.

"Wow." He couldn't imagine what she'd been through, how much it'd pained her to see her husband with someone new, then lose her business on top of it. His heart stirred with sympathy for her.

She studied the horizon with lips pressed in a firm line, nostrils flared. "Yeah, wow is right."

"I'm sorry."

She gave a hollow chuckle. "Honestly, I'm sick of even hearing the words come from my own mouth. I feel like it's the story of my life now, and I don't want it to be any more. I want to write my own story, something better than that. Something amazing. Not pitiful."

He sighed. "I hear you on that one."

She flashed him a smile. "I'm sorry. I didn't mean..."

"No, you're right. I want a less pitiful story too, at least the ending. We should both work on that, better endings."

They laughed together, breaking the tension of the moment.

A pair of plovers called their objection to the couple's intrusion. They scurried toward the drier sand, the air echoing with their cries. A wave crashed against the shore, then hurried toward their horses, slipping around the horses' hooves with quiet bubbles, leaving a trace of froth in the sand before returning to the ocean.

"How is Jennifer?" asked Liz.

He shrugged. "She's... stuck. I spoke to her earlier, I was supposed to spend today with them, and she said they're too busy. Can you believe it? Too busy to see me on Christmas Eve." His blood boiled again at the memory.

"Is it always like that?" asked Liz. "Like it was at the picnic? With Neil?"

Rob's throat tightened, ached. "Yes. He's an angry man. Doesn't treat Jen or the children right. And there's nothing I can do about it." He sighed, rubbed a hand over his face.

"She won't leave him?"

"No, she won't leave him."

"Do you think she's happy?" asked Liz, surprising him.

He thought for a moment. "She says she is, but I know her too well. She's unhappy, afraid..." Thinking about it pushed his heart rate up until its pounding rang in his ears.

"She won't do anything about it, you know, until she's ready to admit she's unhappy. If she won't admit something is wrong, she won't leave him."

Rob sat in silence, pondering her words. She was right, of course. Jen had to make the choice herself, he couldn't make it for her. No matter how much it pained him, he had to wait for her to reach the decision to leave Neil on her own.

❧ 9 ❧

L iz's horse plodded through the sand. She let it have
its head and the reins lengthened in her hands, slipping through her fingers. Rob was lost in thought
and she'd left him to it. He had a lot on his mind and seemed
to need some time to himself. She couldn't blame him; she
couldn't imagine what he must be feeling about his daughter
and the situation she was in. One of the hardest things about
being a parent was letting go of control and watching your
child make mistakes, watching them go through pain, unable
to protect them.

She reached the end of the cove and her horse stopped.
The sand ended there, replaced by black rocks that climbed
from the sand to an outcropping where waves pounded and
leapt high in the air. Another large rock stood apart from the
rest, surrounded by ocean water, like a sentinel just off the
beach.

Some of the other guests had climbed down from their
horses' backs and were picking their way over the rocks,
bending to examine small pools of seawater, or talking

together about the gathering clouds that had begun to darken the sky.

Liz threw a leg over the saddle, then slid to the ground. It was further than she'd thought, and her feet had pins and needles when they hit the hard sand. She let the reins fall to the ground, as the others had done, watched her horse for a few moments. Satisfied that it had no intention of moving, she clambered onto the rocks. She picked her way over their sharp, black edges, grateful she'd worn her runners.

She bent at the edge of one rock pool to study a group of colourful shells. Then, pushed her hand into the warm water to pick one up. A crab tucked its legs quickly into the hidden places of the shell, and she chuckled before replacing the shell in the water. Soft seaweed waved with the movements of the water in another, much larger pool. She ran her fingers through it, enjoying the sensation against her skin.

The last time she'd felt such peace... well, she couldn't remember when it'd been, but it was years ago. Before everything in her life had begun to unravel. Back when she was oblivious to the cliff face, she was rushing toward. When she'd naively believed everything would stay the way it was, forever. How had she failed to see the warning signs that nothing in her life was as she thought?

Perhaps it wasn't entirely Cam's fault. Maybe she could've done some things differently, been more open, more aware of him. He'd said she ignored him, gave everything to the children and forgot about his needs. Maybe he was right. His words had aggravated her no end at the time. How dare he accuse her of ignoring his needs? What about *her* needs? She was a mother, her needs came last, his needs should too. She'd been raising their children. Didn't that count for something?

Still, in hindsight, she could see it. She'd given them every bit of her love, leaving none in her tank—for him or anyone else. Even her friends had accused her of that. How could she have done it any differently though? It was how she was made —to love her children was like breathing air. Loving a husband was another matter entirely. Especially one as selfish as Cam had been. And that's what it boiled down to. She'd ignored it for years, but perhaps all along she hadn't wanted to give him her whole heart, since she knew he'd take it and not give in return. Though she'd never have admitted it at the time.

She'd seen her life as a fairy tale, the perfect husband, children, home, career. Everything she'd worked for was all in her reach. And then, when it fell apart, she'd wailed at the injustice of it all. But looking back, though it hurt to admit, she could see the cracks in that perfect veneer.

Tears wet the corners of her eyes but didn't fall. Pain escaped from her heart where it'd been locked up for so long. Release welled up, pushing a smile onto her face.

Maybe she shouldn't have aimed for perfect after all.

Overhead, dark clouds swirled, and the first fat drop of rain landed on her cheek. She squinted at the threatening sky pregnant with rain.

Echoing her thoughts, Jack yelled to the group. "Saddle up, time to head back folks!"

She smiled, watching as Jack helped each of the guests into their saddles, one by one. She caught her horse easily by the reins and grunted her way into the saddle. Pleased at being able to do it on her own. It'd been years since she'd ridden, but the memories of it seemed to have stuck with her. She'd had years of lessons as a girl, and memories of galloping through open fields, her heart full of joy. Being on horseback again felt familiar, comfortable.

Just then, a flash of lightning lit up the sky nearby, followed rapidly by a crack of thunder so loud it elicited a gasp from the group. Liz held the reins firm as her horse skittered sideways a little.

She stroked the animal's neck. "There, there, just a little thunder. Let's get back to the stables, huh?"

A shout spun her in her saddle. She watched a rider galloping down the beach for a single moment before realising it was Rob. His horse had taken off in the direction of the inn. His arms flailed in the air on either side, his body bounced dangerously to the left, then the right, as the horse careened along the beach.

Without thinking, she spun her horse around, leaned forward and pushed the animal into a gallop after him. The horse's hooves pounded the damp sand. She stood slightly in the saddle, reins gathered in her hands, eyes fixed on Rob's back. He jerked like a puppet on a string, as his horse stumbled in the deeper sand.

She caught him easily when his horse slowed to a trot. She grabbed the reins that'd fallen from Rob's hands, and pulled the animal to a halt. Rob's face was pale.

"You okay?" she asked.

He swung a leg over the animal's back and slid to the ground. She did the same, finding herself face to face with him.

He threw his arms around her shoulders and pulled her close, surprising her.

"Thank you," he said.

Her throat tightened. "Sure... of course. It's nothing."

"No, it's not nothing." He cleared his throat, taking a step back. His eyes found hers. "Thank you. For listening... for being a friend... for coming after me just now."

She nodded, unable to speak for a moment.

"Being flung about like a rag doll on that horse's back, I realised something," he continued. "I can't control everything."

She laughed, shook her head. "I know what you mean. Painful, isn't it?"

He nodded, laughing. "Horrible."

❧ 10 ☙

Rob stared at the phone, inhaled a sharp breath, then picked up the handset. A dial tone buzzed in the air. Rain pounded on the roof, filling the room with its comforting din. He'd recovered from the horse-riding incident, showered and now sat on his bed, dressed, ready for Christmas Eve dinner.

He wanted to call, to try one more time to see his family. He dialled Jen's number, then pushed the phone to his ear as it rang.

Almost ready to hang up, he finally heard Jen's thin voice on the other end of the line.

"Jen?"

"Oh, hi Dad."

"How are you?"

She hesitated. "I'm fine. We're fine. Great... we're great."

His eyes narrowed. They weren't great. He might not be the most intuitive man, but even he knew something was very wrong in Jen's life, whether she was ready to admit it or not.

"I'm glad to hear it," he lied. He hesitated. "Jen, what's going on?"

She didn't respond. Was she sobbing? It was hard to tell because of the rain, pummelling the tin roof overhead.

"Tell me something, honey. Are you happy? If I know you're happy, I'll let it go, but I can't bear for you to be miserable. You're my girl..." His throat ached at a memory of her toddling through the back yard, squealing in delight at the sight of a butterfly as it bobbed and fluttered from one flower to another.

"Is anyone happy, Daddy?"

Her words tore at his heart. "Yes, honey. Some people are... I was..."

"You and Mum, that was different. You had something special..."

"And that's what I want for you," he said.

"What if I can't have that? What if it's not possible?"

He swallowed. "It is honey, it is possible..."

"Dad, I...," her voice changed, brightened. "Yes, we're fine, Dad. Thanks for calling. I'd better go now. Bye."

Again, the dial-tone buzzed in his ear. He stared at the phone a moment, then hung up with a sigh. He should go over there and drag her and the kids away. But then what? It wouldn't change anything. He'd only make things worse.

What should he do?

It was Christmas Eve. He was dressed in a button-down shirt, and a pair of slacks and had even combed his hair with a little gel. He didn't want to be alone. He headed downstairs. The rain had slowed, and the din was not quite so deafening as it had been.

He wandered through the inn, stopping in the sitting room to flip through the pages of a book, his mind elsewhere. Then, he followed the sound of voices into the dining room.

The scent of roasted meat and gravy was heavy in the air. His stomach clenched with sudden hunger, and he licked his lips. Guests were seated around the long dining table at the centre of the room, all dressed in their best summer outfits. The table was decorated with greenery, no doubt plucked from the inn's grounds. Along with sprigs of wattle, some seashells and tea candles. Place settings in silver and red with red Christmas crackers lined both sides of the table.

Mima hovered at one end of the table, holding a carving knife in one hand as she prodded a large turkey with a fork. She looked up, then caught his eye and winked. He smiled.

Mima waddled over to greet him, a grin lighting up her face. "Mr. Patch, how nice to see you this evening."

"Hi, Mima, this looks amazing."

"Are you joining us?" she asked.

He shook his head. "I didn't RSVP."

She waved a hand as if to dismiss his words. "Oh, never mind about that. There's plenty to go around. You should join us."

"Really?" The last thing he wanted to do was go back to his quiet room alone and stare at the television screen as his stomach growled.

"Absolutely. I'll get another place setting for you... there's room at the end there, next to Liz."

"Thank you, Mima."

She squeezed his forearm with one hand. "Merry Christmas, Rob."

He nodded. "Merry Christmas to you as well, Mima."

She ambled toward the kitchen while he made his way to the end of the table. Liz looked up as he pulled out his chair. Her hair shone in the candlelight, and she wore minimal, but elegant makeup that highlighted her cheekbones; her emerald green, sleeveless gown perfectly accentuated her lithe figure and tanned neck.

"Rob, are you staying?"

He nodded and slid into the chair.

She smiled. "Oh wonderful. I'm glad you're eating with us."

His heart warmed at the look on her face. She was genuinely glad to see him, and he found himself wishing he could kiss her pink lips. A feeling that surprised him.

"I'm glad too."

He didn't want to talk about Jennifer or the kids, Neil, or the fact that his Christmas Eve plans had been cancelled and was grateful she didn't ask. Instead, they fell into an easy conversation about horse riding, comparing their experiences and laughing over mishaps.

They ate a crab salad for their appetiser. It was delicious, light, and the Asian dressing lit up Rob's tastebuds. Then, the turkey, roast vegetables, and gravy for a more traditional Christmas Eve meal. It was warm, comforting, and filled Rob so that he thought he might have to loosen his pants. When dessert came, pavlova with fresh whipped cream and slices of tropical fruit, he sighed with satisfaction.

Liz picked up her Christmas cracker and held it out toward him. He smiled and took one end. They both pulled, the cracker string broke with a bang, and he ended up with the larger half. He fished about inside and pulled out a paper crown and pushed it onto his head with a laugh.

They popped his cracker as well, and Liz found a matching crown in it that she set on her own head. They laughed together over the spectacle they made.

"I know it's selfish," said Liz with a grin. "But I'm glad you're here. Otherwise, I'd have no one to share my Christmas Eve with."

"Me too," he replied.

Their gazes connected and he didn't look away. Instead, he wondered what it might be like to fall in love again. He'd thought that part of his life was over and hadn't planned to meet someone who made his heart race the way it was. Not again. Twice in one lifetime seemed too much to hope for. But what did it mean? She lived in Sydney, he in Brisbane. They barely knew each other, yet she felt so familiar to him. Still, even if she felt the same way, which he wasn't convinced she did, how could it work between them? And what would it mean for his carefully constructed life?

❧ II ❧

25TH DECEMBER 1996

CABARITA BEACH

L iz rolled over in bed and scrunched the pillow over her head. The sound of birdsong had woken her off and on for about four hours now. It got light so early in summer, around four a.m., and she'd done her best to sleep late, but to no avail.

It was Christmas morning, and she had nowhere to be.

She turned onto her side and squeezed her eyes shut. She'd never been much good at sleeping late, but if she was going to, today would be the day. Nowhere to go. Nothing to do. No one to see.

She sighed and buried her head in her pillow.

She heard a door shut nearby. Rob's door. He was heading over to see his family today and she hoped for his sake that nothing would get in the way of them having a lovely time together. He deserved some time with the grandchildren, and she hoped Neil wouldn't make it too difficult for him.

All throughout the inn, doors opened and shut as the time ticked by on the clock. Liz stayed in bed, her eyes shut, willing herself to fall back to sleep to pass the time.

By nine am, the inn was silent. It seemed every guest there had somewhere to be, other than her.

Merry Christmas, Liz.

Her eyes blinked open and she grimaced and pressed both hands to her face. She might as well get up and go for a walk along the beach. There was no point staying in bed if she couldn't fall back to sleep. Besides, it was getting hotter outside by the minute, she'd left it too late already to walk without getting sunburned.

Liz dressed in shorts and a long-sleeved shirt then, covered her face in sunscreen and donned a wide-brimmed hat. The oppressive heat assailed her as soon as she stepped outside. Humidity bathed her skin in sweat. The whole world sparkled clean and bright after the rainfall the day before. The grass was greener, the sky bluer. Everything was freshly washed. A pair of curlews scrambled out of her way, disappearing into the undergrowth as she headed down the well-worn trail toward the cove, four small chicks hurrying after them, oversized heads bobbing.

She smiled at the chicks and paused to watch them until she couldn't see them any longer, then she stepped down the timber stairs and into the sand.

Setting a steady pace, Liz strode down the beach. Sweat trickled down the sides of her face and wet her body. She pushed herself to move faster, pumping her arms as she paced. As long as she kept moving, she could stop from thinking about the fact that it was Christmas Day and she was all alone.

Was it so bad?

She'd been dreading this moment for weeks, wondering how it would feel to be on her own, when all around the world people were gathered together, laughing, celebrating, enjoying each other's company.

She gazed down the length of the beach, over the rocks, and out to the heaving ocean. The beauty of the cove always filled her with a sense of peace, of thankfulness. Maybe it wasn't so bad to be on her own after all. She could do this. She could manage it. And once it was behind her, being alone wouldn't be so frightening or something to be dreaded. Instead, she could face it and keep going, maybe even find some joy in it if only for a moment.

Back at the inn, she slumped into a chair in the dining room, fanning her face with one hand. The dining room was empty. Most of the staff had the morning off and someone had left cereal, fruit, yoghurt and toast out for guests to make if they wanted breakfast at the inn.

Liz poured herself a bowl of cereal, covered it with cold milk, and sat at the table alone, crunching on cereal as she stared out the large, rectangular window that dominated one wall of the room. Brilliantly coloured red flowers peeped through, backed by the waving branches of a wattle tree and the steady reaching limbs of a grove of pandanus. Rainbow lorikeets landed in a wattle with a rush of beating wings, then set about stripping its flowers of their nectar. Liz watched with her breath caught in her throat. The brilliant colours of their feathers—green, blue, red, yellow—blended with the wattle. She studied them as she ate and they climbed over the bending limbs of the bush, then, they were gone again in a flurry of bright feathers.

Liz sighed, finished her bowl of cereal, and carried it to the kitchen. A staff member, washing dishes, took it from her with a nod of thanks.

She climbed the stairs, sorrow creeping into her heart.

She missed Macy, her dog. Missed home. Why had she come here? It'd been a bad idea. Though she was grateful for meeting Robert, she should be at home, surrounded by her own things. It was strange to be here, away from home, at this time of year. She stopped at the top of the staircase, turned to lean on the railing and gaze out over the open living room. The Christmas tree near the front door stood regal and proud. An array of colourful ornaments lined its branches, along with a string of white twinkle lights. Beneath it, colourfully wrapped boxes were arranged in neat piles.

With a sigh, she returned to her room to shower and change. By the time she'd finished applying her makeup, the shuttle was there. It idled outside, the driver waiting by the front door as Liz stepped through. She'd booked a Christmas lunch for one at the Charona hotel in Coolangatta. She braced herself and stepped into the shuttle, smiling briefly at the other passengers, before finding a seat on her own.

The hotel was decorated with tasteful elegance and soft Christmas music murmured beneath the hum of conversation. Cinnamon and nutmeg scented the air, and everywhere Liz looked there was a Christmas tree or Santa Claus decorating every available space.

Lunch involved various forms of seafood, including swordfish, crab, prawns, and scallops. The food was beautifully cooked, drizzled in lemon juice and butter, and served alongside fresh and colourful salads that set her tastebuds dancing.

She sat alone, at a table for one, overlooking the beach. Every other table held a couple or a crowd. She watched them a while, then pulled a book from her purse to read while she ate.

After a dessert of lemon curd and ice cream, along with a creamy coffee, Liz rode in the shuttle back to the inn. In her room, she kicked off her shoes, climbed onto the bed and flicked on the television set. It didn't take long to find a

Christmas movie, and she settled back on the mound of pillows to watch.

When the phone rang, she stared at it in surprise a moment before answering it.

"Hello?"

"Merry Christmas, Mum!" shouted Danita with a laugh.

Liz smiled, her heart flooding with love. "Merry Christmas my darling. I didn't think I'd hear from you. How's Austria?"

"We're having the best time. It's beautiful here. A white Christmas—everything is sparkling, clean and white. The mountain is amazing. We've been skiing every day... I love it!"

Liz's throat tightened. "I'm so glad, Dani. I miss you, but I'm happy you're having such a wonderful time. Enjoy it."

They spoke for a few minutes, then Liz hung up the phone, a smile lingering on her face. She'd barely had time to get back into the movie before it rang again. This time it was David, and he wanted to tell her all about Tasmania. He loved it there and thought they should visit it together soon. It sounded like things were getting serious between him and his girlfriend, and Liz found herself taken off guard by how fast her son was moving. He was in love and he wasn't holding any part of himself back. He reminded her of herself, many years earlier. It brought tears to her eyes when he described everything with such enthusiasm and told her he missed and loved her.

She set the earpiece back in its cradle again and stared off into the distance, her heart aching with happiness. Even though she couldn't be with them, she was grateful for her children and their wide-open hearts. She and Cam must've done something right in raising them.

When the phone rang again, she switched off the television and sat up straighter on the bed before answering.

Ivy wished her Merry Christmas, then regaled her with a

tale of her young granddaughter tripping on a step and putting her teeth through her lip sending them all to the emergency room for the entirety of Christmas morning.

Finally, it was Margot's turn. She called soon after Liz hung up with Ivy. Liz could hear yelling in the background.

"What's going on over there?" she asked.

Margot huffed. "They're fighting over a card game. It's ridiculous. Honestly. Frank gets around his brother and I swear he reverts back to childhood. I can't get him to see sense. He's impossible."

Liz chuckled. "I'm sorry, hon."

"Ah... forget it. I've decided to leave him to his own devices and just stay out of the way. Tell me about you, how are you coping with everything? Feeling any better than you were the last time we spoke?"

Liz nodded as she answered. "I am actually. It's strange, I keep expecting to feel sad, being alone on Christmas, but I feel okay. It is quiet, but I'm keeping busy and I really think I'm learning to be on my own, in a way I never have in my life before. Honestly, it feels kind of liberating. Though, of course, I'd kill to have all of you here with me now."

"I get it. You're in a transition period in your life. Things have changed. You were a busy working mum, living with constant chaos, and now you're not. It's different, it's new, and change can be hard to adapt to at first. The fact that you're alone today doesn't mean you're alone in your life, though. You know that, right?"

Liz nodded slowly. "Yeah, I guess you're right."

"You've got us, me and Ivy. You have David, Dani and your parents. As well as dozens of other people who care about you. Being alone at Christmas doesn't mean you're on your own forever."

Liz sighed. "That's true."

"And I'm proud of you for facing this. You're amazing, you know that?"

"Thanks." She didn't feel amazing. She felt like a scared, weak woman who'd struggled to face reality for so long she didn't even know how.

"For so long you've built your life around other people, your husband, your kids, your clients. Now you have to build a new life, one that doesn't revolve around them anymore. It's hard to do, but in the end we all have to face it. I'm married, but I've had to deal with the same thing, creating a new life in this different phase. Life changes, we go through seasons, and this is a new season for both of us."

When she hung up the phone this time, after Margot reminded her that she and Ivy would be in Cabarita Beach soon, Liz lay on the bed, arms behind her head, staring at the ceiling for a long time. Margot was right, as usual, it was a new season, one she'd have to learn to embrace if she was going to move on with her life.

A roast chicken sagged in the middle of the table. Half eaten bowls of potato salad, Caesar salad, grilled prawns, and some kind of quinoa dish formed a half circle around the chicken.

Rob set down his fork and pushed his chair back from the table.

"That was delicious," he said.

He smiled at Jen, nodded in Neil's direction. Tension crept up the back of his neck. He could already feel the muscles in the back of it seizing up. He'd have knots in his shoulders tonight, too bad he hadn't thought to bring his shoulder massager with him. Perhaps he'd book a massage tomorrow at the inn. He saw something about spa treatments in Kingscliff when he'd checked into the Waratah.

Neil ignored him, focused on eating from his second piled helping of Christmas lunch. Rob was grateful for that. The last thing he wanted today was to garner Neil's attention. All he had to do was make it through the day without causing any kind of friction. So far, he'd managed it.

Daniel tapped on Rob's knee. He smiled at the boy and

pushed his chair out a little further. Daniel climbed onto his leg, nestled against Rob's chest.

"Can we play soccer, Grandpa?"

Rob grinned. Already Daniel was mad for the game. He loved nothing more than to tear around the backyard after the white ball, tapping it with his small feet as he went.

"Let's do it," replied Rob.

He swept Daniel up into his arms and tossed him over one shoulder as he headed for the back door. Daniel squealed and kicked in delight, giggling so hard he could barely draw breath.

They passed Sophie, who was outside already. She stood beside a plastic kitchen, broken in places where the sun had weakened the structure, making the plastic brittle. She held a teacup in one hand and a saucer in the other and was talking to a line-up of teddy bears and dolls seated on the patio beside her. Her earnest voice brought a smile to his face.

"Want to play soccer with us, Sophie?" he asked.

She set down the teacup. "Yeah!" She tore after him, her red-striped Christmas dress flying up behind her, her little legs pumping. She'd ditched the matching white sandals hours ago.

He found the soccer ball in a patch of long grass by the back fence and soon the three of them were engaged in an epic and very serious battle to get the ball either between the legs of the swing-set, or through the space between the rusting Weber grill and the weathered trampoline.

While they played, Rob glanced every now and then at the house, through the glass sliding door. He could hear shouts, wondered what was going on. Ever since he'd arrived for Christmas lunch he'd been on tenterhooks. Jen was nervous, her lips twitching back and forth between a smile and downturned. He thought he'd seen a bruise on her temple, but it was hard to say since she was wearing more makeup today than she usually would. In fact, with her olive complexion and naturally pretty features, she rarely wore makeup, or any kind of embellishments. She was naturally beautiful like her mother.

Was it possible Neil wasn't only a grumpy, obnoxious man, but violent as well? Rob didn't want to believe it. Surely Jen wouldn't stay in the home if he was hurting her. And what about the children?

Just then, Sophie kicked the ball through the swing set, then leapt into his arms with a shout of triumph. Daniel slumped onto the ground, tears in his eyes, fists clenched into balls.

"No, not fair!" he cried. "Not fair!"

Rob held her close, inhaling the fresh scent of her hair as he kissed her round cheek. She laughed, eyes sparkling. "Did you see, Grandpa? Did you see?"

He chuckled. "I saw. You were absolutely amazing. A little Maradona."

"A what?" she asked, her brow creasing in confusion.

He shook his head. "Never mind." He set her feet back on the ground and ruffled her hair with one hand.

No, it couldn't be true, the kids seemed fine. They were happy, healthy, completely oblivious to whatever was going on inside the house. It'd quietened down now, but the silence bothered him almost more than the noise had.

He scooped Daniel into his arms and comforted the little boy with a turn on the swing. Daniel soon forgot all about the lost soccer match and asked to be pushed higher and higher.

"Who's ready to open presents?" he asked.

Sophie and Daniel both snapped to attention, eyes fixed on his face, smiles widening.

"Me! Me!"

"I am!"

He laughed, took each child by the hand, and led them

into the house. "Now, I had too many snails in my garden, so I hope you both like snails..."

Daniel's brow furrowed. "I do, Grandpa. I love 'em."

Sophie's blue eyes narrowed. "Grandpa. You didn't wrap snails."

He laughed. "I can't get anything past you, Sophie my darling. You're too smart for me."

Jen was in the kitchen, putting the last of the leftovers away in the fridge. Her cheeks were red, her eyes watery. She wiped her eyes with the back of one hand when she saw them, pushed a smile onto her face with a sniffle.

"Oh hi. How was soccer?"

Daniel reached for her and she picked him up, squeezed him against herself.

Rob watched her, anger stirring in his gut. "Are you okay?"

She nodded, still smiling. "I'm fine."

"You're crying?"

She shook her head. "Just happy to see the three of you. I'm glad you're here, Dad. I missed you."

Sophie stared at her mother in silence, her face reflecting curiosity and wariness. Jen reached out a hand to squeeze her daughter's shoulder.

"Did you get a goal, honey?" she asked.

Sophie nodded. "I won the game. I beat Grandpa and Danny."

"Wow, you're amazing." Jen sniffled again.

"Where's Neil?" asked Rob, his stomach churning and a pulse pounding in his ears. He wanted a word with the man who was mistreating his daughter. See how he liked facing up to another man. See how he liked being confronted about his cowardice.

"He's asleep in the lounge room," she said, her eyes fixed on his, almost begging him. "Please Dad, leave it. Don't start anything, it's fine. We're all fine. He's asleep, let's have a nice time together. I hardly get to see you..."

"And whose fault is that?" hissed Rob.

"Shhh..." Jen's eyes widened, her gaze darting toward the lounge room doorway.

Rob shook his head. "Let's all take a walk down to the park. That way Daddy can have a sleep and we can talk in peace and quiet." He arched an eyebrow in Jen's direction.

Worry flitted over her features. "I don't know..."

"Come on, we can't exactly keep the kids quiet in the house. If they wake up Neil..."

Her lips pressed into a firm line. "I suppose that's true. But if he wakes up and we're not here..."

"What? What happens then, Jen? If he wakes up and you're not here, what will he do?" Rob hated pushing her, hated the way it made her face scrunch up as though she was in pain. But what else could he do? How could he get her to confront what was going on in her life? To do something about it?

"I suppose you're right," she ignored his questions. "Let's all go to the park," she said in a hushed voice.

"Yay!" cried Daniel, wriggling from her grasp.

"Shhh..." she admonished the retreating back of her son as he scrambled for the front door. "Get your hats please, and shoes!"

As they walked along the footpath toward the park, with each house they passed Rob's anxiety levels rose. He knew what he had to do. It was time to talk frankly with his daughter about her life choices. Still, how to say it? If only Martha were there, she'd know what to say. If Martha were there, they'd never have gotten into this situation because Jen wouldn't have married Neil. At least, that's what he'd always believed.

If Martha had been around when Jen had met Neil, she

would've known who her daughter was dating and might have done something about it. Rob had been mired in such a haze of grief over losing his wife, he hadn't even realised Jen was seeing someone until it was too late.

Even if he'd been in a place to say something about it, what would he have said? He didn't have the kind of close relationship with Jen that Martha had. The two of them had done everything together, they'd been inseparable. He could still hear their laughter sometimes, ringing from the living room when he was preparing food in the kitchen. It was a ghost of a laugh now, but for a moment he'd believe Martha and Jen were thick as thieves in the other room and everything was back the way it had been. It didn't happen as often these days, but for a few years after her death, he'd had snatches of time where he forgot she was gone and thought he heard or saw her.

Martha and Jen talked about everything. They enjoyed the same books, movies, music, and art. They loved attending gallery openings and would critique the food at restaurants in the same way. They both did impressions of celebrities and would have him and each other in stitches of laughter over their take on Jack Nicholson, or Michael Douglas.

He'd sit back and watch, a grin on his face. Happy to see the two of them get along so well. He wasn't in on the secrets, wasn't part of the conversation. A lot of the time he was at work, while the two of them grew their friendship and built their intimacy. He missed it all. So busy working on white papers, getting research grants, publishing his findings. And now, he wished he could change it all. Wished with everything he had, that he'd focused more on building the kind of relationship with his daughter that would encourage her to share things with him, tell him what was wrong, give him a chance to help her through it. Only he didn't have that kind of relationship with Jen, because he hadn't built it when she was young. Was it too late now?

They reached the park and Daniel raced immediately for the sandpit. He dropped to his knees and began digging in the sand. Sophie headed for the swings. She was big enough to swing herself now, she'd proudly told him the last time they were at the park together. She didn't need his help. It happened so fast, this independence. If you weren't careful, they'd be stepping out on their own before you were ready, before you'd built the kind of foundation to your relationship that would keep them connected.

He watched Sophie pumping her legs, getting the swing moving. He and Jen found a park bench by the sandpit, in the shade of a bottlebrush bush. He lowered himself onto the bench with a grunt.

Jen slid onto the seat beside him, one foot tapping on the ground. She chewed a fingernail, her gaze fixed on Daniel as he dug a hole in the sand with both hands. His brown hair swung into his face as he leaned forward to dig deeper.

"When did you start biting your nails?" asked Rob.

Jen pulled the finger from her mouth, stared at it like it was a foreign object for a moment, then folded it into her lap. "Uh... I don't know."

"Jen..." Rob rested a hand on her arm.

She jumped, then glanced at his hand. Rob pulled it away, an ache building in his throat.

"Jen, I think you should leave Neil." There, he'd said it. Blunt, to the point. Perhaps he could've worked his way up to it, but it'd spilled from his mouth as though the words had a mind of their own.

She met his gaze, a frown pulling her eyebrows together. "What?"

"You should leave him. You and the kids. It isn't safe for you to stay here any longer."

"Yes, it is. We're fine." She snapped the words, wrapping her arms around her body as though she could protect herself that way.

"You're not fine." He reached up to touch her cheek and she started again, wincing when his hand brushed her skin. "That's not normal, Jen, to get a fright like that because someone touches you. It's not fine."

She inhaled a long, slow breath. "What would you have me do, Dad? He's my husband. These are our children. We're a family."

"Is he hitting you?"

She faced him, tears making her eyes gleam. "You don't understand. He's under a lot of stress. Things at work... they're not good. He doesn't mean to do it, he's always sorry..."

"Jen..." he shook his head, the lump in his throat building. "Jen, it doesn't matter how stressful things are. That's not okay."

He wanted to take her in his arms like he had when she was a child. To carry her away from there. Never look back.

She sobbed and the sound tore at his heart. He scooted closer on the bench and wrapped an arm around her thin shoulders. He hadn't realised how thin she'd gotten. The bones of her shoulder blades poked into his arm.

She shuddered a moment, then relaxed against him. "I don't know what to do, Dad. The kids..."

"You leave him, that's what you do. Leave and don't look back."

"It doesn't work that way, Dad. He's their father. Besides, I don't even have a job. I have nothing." She rubbed her face with both hands, sniffling into her palms.

He swallowed. "You can stay with me. Get the kids and come live with me. There's plenty of room..."

She met his gaze, a sliver of hope lighting up her eyes. "Really?"

He nodded. "Of course. You're always welcome."

She offered a wobbly smile. "Thanks Dad. But he'll find us there."

A chill flitted through his body, making him shiver. Were things as bad as that?

"What do you mean? What will he do if he finds you?"

She shrugged but didn't answer.

৩৯৫

THE SUN WAS SETTING BEHIND HIM WHEN HE PULLED INTO the parking lot at the inn. He'd left Jen's house hours earlier, then gone to the beach to take a walk and think things through. He opened the car door and stepped out into the humid evening.

A cool breeze riffled his hair for a moment, then fell away, pushed out by the oppressive heat once more. A curlew called in the distance, its mournful cry sending goose bumps over his back. Pink shafts of light reached across the sky, turning blue to purple. The first stars blinked overhead.

Inside the inn, a few lights were on. Cicadas set up a chorus outside. Otherwise the night was quiet.

He headed into the inn and greeted Bindi who was looking over some books at a small desk she kept near the reception counter. She smiled and waved hello and wished him a Merry Christmas. He responded in kind and kept moving.

The stairs got his blood pumping, but he stopped halfway up. He didn't want to go to his room, not yet. He wanted to be around people for a few more minutes before he buried himself in solitude. People who weren't in danger, people who could carry on a normal conversation. He was bursting with the emotion of the day. If he couldn't find someone to talk with, maybe he should find a book to take to bed with him.

What he really wanted, was to find Liz. So, when he saw her in the sitting room, her legs tucked up beneath her, bare feet poking out from under a pair of shorts, her hair pushed behind her ears, and a book open in her lap, he almost laughed.

"Liz, there you are. Merry Christmas!"

She glanced up at him and smiled. "Merry Christmas, Rob. I hope you had a nice day."

He slumped into the chair beside her. "Uh... well. Yeah."

She closed her book, faced him. "I'm here, if you want to talk about it."

He scrubbed both hands over his face with a sigh. "I told her she should leave him."

"You did? How did she take it?"

He was relieved Liz didn't condemn him for it. All the way home he'd been wondering if he'd done the right thing or made everything worse, harder for his daughter to bear.

"She seemed open to the idea. At least a little. She's worried he'll come after them."

Liz leaned back in her chair. "Wow. That's hard. I'm sorry, Rob."

He shook his head. "I know. She's under so much stress. I don't know how she manages... she's so strong." His voice broke. "I don't know what to do, what to say to her. I feel like I'm getting it all wrong."

Liz reached for his arm, squeezing it. "You're not getting it all wrong, you're caring about her. That's what matters."

His heart warmed at the look of compassion on Liz's face. He set his hand over hers, cupping it against his arm. "Thanks, Liz. It means a lot to me."

She smiled. "Of course. You're a good father. She's a wonderful woman. You'll work this thing out between you."

He inhaled a sharp breath. "I hope so. I'm really getting worried. I didn't realise how bad things have gotten. I shouldn't have stayed away for so long, but I thought I was giving her some breathing room, a chance to work on things. That me being around made things worse. I shouldn't have stayed away..."

"Don't blame yourself," admonished Liz. "This is all on Neil, it's his fault. It's not Jen's and it's not yours. You're doing what you think is best, you can't do anything more than that. You're right. She should leave him, and she should do it sooner rather than later."

Her words soothed him and helped some of the spinning thoughts to still in his mind.

"I know what we need," she said, her feet sliding to the ground. "Hot chocolate."

He laughed. "It's the middle of summer!"

"That makes no difference. When things are hard, hot chocolate is always the answer." She winked, stood to her feet, and slipped her sandals back on.

He followed her to the kitchen. It was dark, with only a few small lights glowing at intervals around the room.

"Are we allowed to do this?" he asked as she began opening and closing cupboard doors.

"Mima said we should help ourselves. There aren't any staff on tonight, so we're on our own. Now, where did she say the mugs were? Ah, here they are."

Liz pulled two white mugs from the cupboard, set them next to the jug, then flipped the switch to make it boil. She folded her arms over her chest and smiled at him while they waited.

"I forgot to ask, how was your day?" he said.

She shrugged. "It was fine. I had lunch in Coolangatta. Ate some lobster. It was delicious."

He smiled. "That sounds nice. Relaxing... unlike my day."

He chuckled. "Although, I'm glad I got to spend time with Sophie and Daniel. They really are a gorgeous couple of kids."

She nodded. "They definitely are."

"Did you take a walk?" he asked.

"Yes, I had a nice walk on the beach, and I spoke to my kids, my friends... it was lovely actually, everyone called to wish me well."

The jug finished boiling and she scooped chocolate mix into each of the mugs, then poured the water over it.

"Good," he said.

She nodded. "I wasn't expecting it, in fact, I was kind of dreading today. But in the end, it wasn't so bad. I suppose not every Christmas has to look the same. And I have to admit, there were a lot of Christmas's back when I was younger when I would've loved to have a few minutes sitting in a comfortable chair with my feet up and no children nagging me." She laughed. "Christmas used to mean me feeding dozens of people, on my feet all day cooking, washing dishes, serving people, chasing children. After years of all that, I suppose I should be grateful to have a quiet, relaxing day, with no one else to take care of."

He smiled. "That's the spirit."

Rob reached for Liz's hand without thinking, it was an impulse, almost as though it were natural for him to do it. He picked up her hand and threaded his fingers through hers, studying the length of her fingers, the pink of her nail polish, the way her tanned skin looked against his pale hand.

As she responded, sliding her hand into his, a tingle ran down his arm and over his body. He glanced up, her eyes were fixed on him, her cheeks pink. He didn't say a word, simply smiled and she returned the gesture, as warmth flooded his heart.

🪰 13 🪰

26TH DECEMBER 1996

CABARITA BEACH

A wave slapped at the black rocks at the end of the cove, sending sea spray into the air. With a hiss, the wave retreated back into the ocean. Liz watched, a smile tickling the corners of her mouth. She'd miss this place when she left.

Now that Christmas was over, she felt a sense of relief. She'd faced a Christmas alone, and she'd managed to come through it, even enjoyed it. She was glad she'd come to the Waratah inn after all. Especially since having met Robert. She hoped that talking to her had helped him process everything going on in his family.

Remembering the previous evening, when they'd shared hot chocolates together in the dark kitchen set her heart racing. He'd held her hand and it'd surprised her. Perhaps she'd misjudged him. Did he see her as something more than a friend? It'd seemed that way, when he wove his fingers through hers and caressed the back of her hand. Even the memory of it sent heat rushing to her cheeks.

Sweat trickled down the middle of her back. She'd walked along the beach, around the end of the cove, and up Cabarita Beach for the past hour. Now, she was ready for a swim.

The cool water looked inviting. Small waves curled lazily toward the sand. She slipped out of her summer dress and let it fall onto the sand. Her simple, red one-piece swimsuit was brighter and more attention grabbing than anything she'd worn in years. Usually, she bought swimsuits in black or navy blue, not wanting to draw attention to herself. The other day, while shopping with Mima and Betty, she'd bought this swimsuit. It was brightly coloured, had a plunging neckline and drew high over each hip.

Mima convinced her to get it, said she should flaunt it while she still had it. Liz argued she wasn't sure she still had anything at all left to flaunt, and Mima had huffed at that and rolled her eyes. "Of course, you do," she'd said. "You're still a spring chicken." Liz had laughed then and decided to buy the swimsuit. After all, Mima was right about one thing—she'd never be younger again than she was at that moment.

She padded toward the water, the wet sand cool against the soles of her feet. The remnants of a wave licked at her legs, and she laughed as the cold of it rose to her thighs, then gasped as she plunged her body into the cold water. She dove under a wave, came up, and scrubbed the hair and water from her eyes.

It felt good to take a swim. Why didn't she do that more often back at home? She lived near the beach, and she should take advantage of it. When she got home, she was going to walk more, swim more, live life more outside of the confines of the four walls of her house.

A man walked toward her. She rubbed her eyes clear of salt water. It was Rob. She waved a hand over her head. He waved back, then slipped his shirt over his head and strode into the water.

Her heart skipped a beat.

He looked fit and strong, his chest firm, his arms thick. She wasn't expecting that from a professor. It brought a smile to her face.

He dove beneath a wave, then swam to where she stood.

"Hi," he said.

She grinned. "Hi."

"Beautiful morning."

"Yes, it is."

The tension between them was palpable. Something unspoken but understood. A shiver of expectation ran through her body.

"Are you okay this morning?" she asked.

He nodded. "Yeah, I guess so. I hope Jen and the kids are fine. I'm worried about them. I thought I might call later to see how she's doing."

"Good idea."

"I think I'm going to talk to her about leaving Neil again. Maybe she's had time to think about it some more. I don't know..."

She nodded. He stood close to her, his body glistening. She pushed a hand into a small wave and flicked water over him.

His eyes widened, he grinned, then flicked her with water. She squealed and dove out of the way. What was she doing? She was acting like a teenager all over again. This wasn't how Elizabeth Cranwell behaved. Yet she found she didn't care and certainly didn't want to stop.

He chased after her, caught her, and dunked her beneath the water. She emerged, laughing, and pushed against him, unable to budge him. She grimaced, he picked her up, held her in the air above him and smiled. Then threw her into the water. She plunged beneath a wave, then stood to her feet, water cascading from her body.

She laughed. "That's not fair, I can't throw you."

He chuckled. "You started it."

They body surfed side by side for a while then took turns catching waves, praising each other over this turn or that tumble. She found herself looking for excuses to touch his arm or stand close to him. Her entire body trembled when she did that. She almost didn't recognise herself anymore and she liked it.

"My friends are arriving tonight. You remember, I told you they decided to visit me, spend a few days at the inn with me?"

He nodded. "I'm looking forward to meeting them. I'm sure you'll have a wonderful time together."

He seemed a little disappointed. She wondered if it was because the two of them wouldn't be alone. She hadn't thought about that but couldn't shake the feeling now. The more she got to know him, the more she wanted to spend time with him, talk to him, laugh with him. Still, she couldn't wait to see Margot and Ivy. She missed her friends so much.

❦

LIZ TURNED TO GET A GLIMPSE OF HER BACK IN THE mirror, then spun the other way. Nerves fluttered in the pit of her stomach. Why was she nervous? It was only Margot and Ivy. Still, she was excited to see them. Their shuttle should be arriving at the inn any moment now.

Darkness crept over the landscape with long shadows surrounding the inn. Liz pulled the curtains shut, then paced to her bed and flicked on the television, flicked it off again, and decided to head downstairs to wait for her friends instead.

She sat in a chair near the front door, her high-heeled feet tapping out a rhythm on the hardwood timber floors.

"Waiting for someone?" asked Bindi, from her place at the reception counter.

Liz nodded. "My friends are arriving tonight."

"That's right. You must be looking forward to seeing them." Bindi grinned. "I hope you have a wonderful time together.'

"Thank you, I'm sure we will. I don't know why I'm nervous." She laughed. "I feel like I'm going on a first date or something."

"You miss them, that's all."

"True."

They were there all in a rush. Margot opened her arms and enveloped Liz in an embrace, a pashmina flapping around her as she regaled Liz on the details of their flight and a particular man on their flight who kept sneezing at the back of her head.

Ivy breezed in, all elegance and long, tanned legs. She kissed Liz on the cheek.

"You've lost weight, chickie." Her eyes sparkled.

"I don't know... maybe. I'm not sure how, all I seem to do here is eat."

"And walk," added Margot, foraging in her purse for something.

"True, I have been walking a lot."

"Good for you. I feel more peaceful already here. Don't you feel peaceful?" She turned to Margot.

Margot peered around the inn, shrugged. "I guess so."

Liz helped them check in and locate their rooms upstairs.

They were both on the second floor, both had lovely rooms—Margot's decorated in navy, silver and white, Ivy's in cream, pale pink, and gold. Somehow the decor matched both their personalities perfectly.

"This place is stunning," mused Margot.

Ivy stood beside her in the bathroom. Both women were checking their makeup. Liz lay on her stomach on the bed, watching them, a smile tugging at the corners of her mouth. She couldn't believe they were there. It had been years since they'd gotten away together as a trio for a holiday.

"This is so nice, I'm glad you decided to come up here with me."

Margot grinned as she opened a tube of lipstick. "I'm glad too. We don't do this often enough. No men, just us—it's going to be great. Where should we go for tea?"

"You must be starving, it's so late. I'm not sure what will be open," mused Liz. "I'll go downstairs and see if Bindi is still around. She'll know."

Bindi guided the three of them to a restaurant and bar in Coolangatta that she said would be open late.

"And besides," she said. "They're not on Daylight Saving time, so they're an hour behind us, which means it's not so late there as it is here."

Liz remarked that it was a strange place where you could drive for half an hour and end up traveling an hour back in time. She ordered a taxi, and by the time it arrived her friends had freshened up and were ready to go.

Out on the porch, she tugged on the edges of her cardigan to pull it tighter around her shoulders. A scratching sound caught her attention, and she gasped as a large, brown possum trundled by clinging to the top railing of the verandah fence.

"What on earth?"

Margot burst through the door, laughing loudly at something Ivy had said, her friend right behind her. She crunched on an apple then adjusted the purse strap on her right shoulder.

"I'm so hungry, I couldn't wait. I think I might faint if I don't get some food into me soon," complained Margot.

The possum wrapped its tail around the verandah railing, reached out both front paws and snatched Margot's apple right out of her hand. Margot gasped and took a stumbling step backward. "What is that?"

"Possum..." muttered Liz by way of explanation. Though she couldn't understand it any better herself. She'd never come across a possum who would walk up to a person and take the apple right out of their hand before.

Ivy stood in silence, her mouth hanging open.

The possum tucked the apple into her mouth and sauntered back down the railing, disappearing into the darkness.

"Well, I never..." sputtered Margot.

"No, never," added Ivy, her voice soft.

The yellow cab's headlights swept across them as the vehicle took the wide circular drive and pulled up in front of the inn. Smoke gusted from the car's tailpipe.

"Let's go then," said Liz.

The three of them bundled into the vehicle, Margot's usual chatter quieted for only a minute or so, then she was back into it with vigour, the stolen apple forgotten.

The restaurant wasn't their usual style, with a live rock band playing in one corner. They found a table as far away from the noise as they could manage, almost buried beneath a tall ficus tree. After ordering their meal of seafood and hot chips, Liz steepled her hands.

"So, you two, tell me what you've been doing. I want to hear all about your holidays."

Margot rolled her eyes. "Nothing changed after I spoke to you last. Frank was mired in competition with his brother for the entire trip, if it wasn't comparing who had the biggest house, it was the best nine-iron, or the most trips to South Africa for business in a year. They couldn't even take a leak without comparing who had the strongest stream. It was ridiculous."

Ivy laughed until her sides hurt as Margot shared story after story of her husband trying to one-up his brother, even ending up with a bruised rib after the two of them decided they could outdo the other free climbing rocks at a picnic one day.

When finally, her laughter waned and her breath returned, Liz faced Ivy with a smile. "And what about you Ivy? How were the Blue Mountains?"

Ivy wiped the tears of laughter from her eyes and pressed her lips into a straight line. "It was fine."

Liz and Margot exchanged a look.

Liz arched an eyebrow. "Fine?"

Ivy adjusted her shirt. "Yes, it was fine. I mean, you know we spent Christmas Day in the emergency room when Jenna split her lip."

Liz nodded. Margot leaned forward in her seat.

Ivy rolled her eyes. "Well, the next day we decided to have a picnic, in the bush. We set up beside this darling little stream. We could hear the water dancing over the stones while we ate."

"Sounds lovely," said Liz.

"Yes, it was. It was beautiful. Well, my son and daughter-in-law have a baby, and they decided to take the kids in the car for a few minutes, to try to get the baby to sleep. She falls asleep in the car, but otherwise... anyway, they bundled into the car and off they went, leaving Steve and I there alone."

Ivy bit down on her lower lip, studied her friends' faces. Her cheeks grew pink.

"So, Steve and I took a walk along the creek. Before long we were far from the picnic site and completely on our own. There was no one around for miles. It was beautiful! We saw all these different birds, butterflies, wildflowers. Anyway, it was hot, and the water looked so inviting."

Liz pressed her lips together to keep from laughing. She had a feeling she knew where the story was going but didn't want to interrupt.

"It was Steve's idea... at least I think it was. Anyway, we both ended up naked in the creek."

Margot burst out with a loud "ha", then sat back in her chair grinning.

"You went skinny dipping?" asked Liz.

Ivy nodded.

"That's not so bad, you've done that before. If I had a figure like yours, I'd skinny dip all the time," mused Liz, her brow furrowed.

Ivy inhaled a sharp breath. "That's not the end of the story..."

Margot laughed again. "Boy, this is gonna be good."

Ivy rolled her eyes. "We swam for a while, splashed each other, had a laugh, fooled about a bit... you know."

Liz nodded. "Sure..."

"Then, we went to get out of the creek, and we realised we'd floated further downstream than we thought we had."

Margot's eyes widened.

Ivy continued. "We couldn't find our clothes. We were completely lost. We hiked back upstream a little way, but our clothes weren't on the bank where we thought we'd find them. It started to get dark, and we knew our family would be looking for us..."

"Oh dear," commented Liz, her eyebrows knitting together.

"Yes, well... we walked in the direction we thought would take us back to the picnic area. When we finally got there, it was dusk, there were groups of people out looking for us everywhere. And here we come, the naked grandparents, trooping into the clearing in front of all the children, the searchers, even the police..."

Margot couldn't hold it in any longer. She whooped with laughter and slapped a hand over her mouth to stifle the noise.

Liz bit down a giggle and pressed a hand to Ivy's arm in sympathy. "Oh honey, I'm sorry. That must've been embarrassing and scary."

Ivy nodded. "And the worst part is, I've got stings, bites and scrapes in places no one ever should..."

That was the final straw. All three of them burst into gales of laughter until tears streamed down their cheeks.

When they finally composed themselves, Liz felt as though she'd run a marathon. Her sides ached, her lips trembled, and she was spent. The food arrived and they all ate with gusto, exchanging small talk for a few minutes. Fried chunks of fresh, moist fish, calamari, scallops grilled in butter, and king prawns, alongside a mound of hot, thick chips. It was delicious and soon filled them up.

Liz gulped a large mouthful of mineral water before leaning back in her chair with a sigh. "That was exactly what I needed."

"I haven't eaten fried food in an age," agreed Ivy, patting her flat stomach.

Margot reached for another chip. "So, Liz, how about you? Tell us what you've been doing up here in paradise the past few days."

"It's been a lot better than I thought it'd be, actually. I've been on a river cruise, ate Christmas lunch at a nice hotel, went horse riding on the beach... really, when I think about it, I've had a lovely time. A lot of that has to do with Rob though."

Both friends leaned forward at the same time. Ivy smiled.

Margot's eyes twinkled. "Rob? Who's Rob?"

Liz sighed. "I knew you'd make more of it than what it is..."

"And what is it?" asked Ivy.

"We're friends. He's a very nice man; he's staying at the inn on his own as well, so we've been doing a lot of things together."

"And?" encouraged Margot.

"And... we're friends. That's all."

"Uh huh." Ivy looked unconvinced.

"He's been having a few issues with his family, so I've been helping him navigate that. Well, I've listened... that's about all I've done really. Still, I think he appreciates it. I know I'm grateful for him, anyway. He helped me get through Christmas."

Ivy and Margot exchanged a look. Margot reached for Liz's hand and squeezed it. "He sounds wonderful, I can't wait to meet him."

"It's not like that," objected Liz. "He lives in Brisbane, and my life is in Dee Why..."

Ivy nodded. "It's complicated. Life is complicated."

"And we haven't talked about anything... we're friends. That's all."

"Has he kissed you?" asked Margot.

Liz shook her head. "No."

"Held your hand?" asked Ivy.

"Well... yes."

Margot looked smug. "There you go."

Liz's brow furrowed. "That doesn't mean anything."

Ivy shrugged.

"You're making more of this... ugh. I knew you'd make more of it than it is. You're both impossible."

"Sorry, honey. That's our job. Anyway, looking forward to meeting this stud," chuckled Margot.

Liz huffed. "Well, I'm sure you'll meet him in the morning. But please don't embarrass me."

"No promises," replied Margot with a wink.

❧ 14 ❧

CABARITA BEACH

R ob raised a fist toward the door, then lowered it to his side again. He inhaled a slow breath, raised his fist again and knocked.

He hadn't called ahead, hoping that if he showed up unannounced perhaps Neil would let him in without thinking about it too much.

He fidgeted with the seam of his jeans while he waited. Footsteps in the hallway, then the door squeaked open.

"Dad?" Jen pulled the door all the way open and stepped aside. "Come on in."

He smiled. "Hey honey. Good to see you again."

"I wasn't expecting you. Neil isn't home."

He gave her a hug, kissed her cheek. "Are the kids here?"

She nodded. "There playing in the living room."

He found them making things out of play dough. Daniel was thumping his lump of dough with a small, timber hammer and Sophie was rolling long ropes of it between her hands, then curling the ropes into snails.

"Grandpa!" exclaimed Sophie, rushing to hug his legs.

He laughed. "Hey sweetheart, good morning Daniel."

Daniel grinned and held up the hammer. "We're making stuff."

"That's great," replied Rob with a wink.

He sat with them for a few minutes, showing them how to make a hamburger, then a car, followed by a sad attempt at a sagging tree.

Finally, he joined Jen in the kitchen where she was pouring both of them cups of coffee.

"Let's take these outside," she suggested.

He picked up the mugs with a dip of his head and followed her through the glass sliding doors to a pair of chairs on the patio outside.

There were dark smudges beneath Jen's eyes. Her hair was lank and oily, her skin pallid.

"Are you okay?" asked Rob as he slid into a chair and took a sip of coffee.

She nodded. "We're all fine."

"You say that a lot. Fine. It's not a great word, Jen. Not a good way to live."

"What do you want me to say, Dad?" she spat.

He raised a hand as if in surrender. "Sorry."

She shook her head. "No, I'm sorry. It's not your fault. I'm tired, that's all."

Rob pursed his lips, drew a deep breath. "It's not fatigue, Jen. It's time you and the kids packed up and left. This isn't a life. It's no way to live. You deserve so much more than this. It breaks my heart to see you living this way."

Jen cradled the coffee cup in her hands, tucked her feet up

beneath her, knees under her chin and stared out into the backyard. "It's not that easy, Dad."

"Yes, it is. You can do it now. Pack up some things while he's gone and leave."

"He went fishing hours ago. He'll be home at any moment..."

"I'll help," he said, setting his coffee cup on a small, round glass table beside him.

She met his gaze. "I don't know."

"It's time for a new start, Jen."

She nodded. "I know it is."

"So, let's do it."

"Okay."

He couldn't believe she'd said the word. Okay. Such a simple word, but it meant so much. She'd finally agreed to leave Neil. He'd been working toward this moment for years. Ever since Daniel was born, and Neil had berated Jen at the hospital for not ordering breakfast for him when she ordered her own. She tried to explain to him that it was only for patients, but he'd been too angry to listen and stormed out, leaving her alone with her newborn and toddler.

That was the moment Rob knew she couldn't stay in the relationship. It wasn't the first time he'd seen Neil mistreat his daughter, but it was the turning point in his view of the man and their marriage.

She found some old suitcases in the garage, stacked on top of a set of shelves. Rob helped her to pack them with things she and the kids would need, along with their favourite toys. The kids watched cartoons on the television in the living room while they worked, oblivious to what was going on.

"What will I tell the children?" asked Jen, her brow creased with worry.

"I don't know, but we'll figure all that out together," replied Rob.

"I think you should go," said Jen, her voice high. She glanced out the bedroom door.

"What? We're almost ready," he replied.

Her eyes widened at a noise. "He'll be back soon. If he sees your car parked on the street, he'll be angry. You should go. Don't worry, I'll find a way to get out of here. If he comes before we leave, I'll wait until he's asleep or something."

"I don't know. I don't want to leave you..."

"If he finds you here, we won't make it. Please Dad. I can't focus, I'm so stressed about him coming back and how angry he'll be."

"But if I'm not here, he could hurt you..." Rob didn't want to leave her and the children alone. Now that she'd agreed to come with him, he couldn't bear the idea of walking away without them.

"No, it'll be okay. I'll hide the suitcases, he won't know. I'll meet you at the inn. All right?"

Rob swallowed. "If you think that's best..."

"I do."

"Okay." He nodded. "I'll see you later, at the inn. We'll drive home together."

As he drove away, Rob's mind churned over the details of the morning. He shouldn't have left her there alone with the kids and three half-packed suitcases. He should've stayed. They could be almost finished by now. Could have the kids buckled in the car. If Neil came home, he could've confronted the man, told him to mind his own business, that the family was coming with him.

Still, perhaps Jen was right. A confrontation wouldn't help anyone. It would only escalate the situation. It was her life, her decision. If she wanted to do it alone, then he'd let her. He only hoped she wouldn't change her mind.

He stopped off at Tweed City and had a duplicate made of his house key to give to Jen. Then, bought a few supplies for her and the kids: some food, juice poppers, toys.

Back at the inn, he got to work making phone calls. He called his neighbour and asked her to check on the house. She called back a few minutes later to say that everything looked fine to her. Then, he called the cleaner to ask her to set up the guest bedrooms in preparation for his guests. She agreed, said she'd do it that afternoon.

After he was done, he packed his own suitcase. Then, sat on the bed, feet crossed, waiting. His fingers drummed on one leg as he waited, his mind racing. He switched on the television and found an old movie to watch, hoping to distract himself.

When the movie finished, he found he'd bitten all his fingernails down to the quick. He glanced at the clock on his bedside table. Five p.m. It was late. He'd left Jen's house hours ago. Where was she?

He dialled her number, but the telephone rang out. No one picked up on the other end. He stared at the phone for a full minute before replacing the handset. Something was wrong.

He tried again, but each time he dialled the telephone rang out. He should go over there. See for himself what was going on. Perhaps Jen was on her way to the inn, or maybe something had happened to her and the kids.

Just then, the phone jangled, startling him out of his reverie. He grabbed up the handset and pressed it to his ear with a sharp intake of breath.

"Jen?"

"Hi Dad."

"Jen, where are you? What happened? I've been waiting here for hours..."

"We're not coming, Dad." Her voice was a whisper, it dripped with resignation.

"What? Why not?"

"He came home, Dad. He saw the suitcases. It was bad." She was whispering still.

His heart fell. "I'm so sorry, honey."

"He's angry, and he's said I can't leave the house. I'm not allowed to answer the phone, but he's watching the news at the moment, so I snuck in here to call you. I can't talk for long..."

"Jen, honey, I'm so sorry."

"It's not your fault, Dad. I should've known better, should have listened. This is my life, my home. I'm stuck here, Dad."

He ran a hand over his hair, tears mounted in his throat. "No, it's not your life. You hear me? Things are going to change. I won't let you live this way..."

"It's not up to you, Dad. I don't know when I'll be able to call again. I love you. Goodbye."

"I love you too. Goodbye," he croaked, as the dial tone rang in his ear.

He hung up the phone, then slumped onto the bed, hands covering his face. What had he done? He'd only wanted to help her, and he'd ended up making things a hundred times worse. It was his fault she was hurting, his fault she was in pain. He groaned against his palms. He had to do something. But what? Perhaps he should call the police. But what if that only further incensed Neil? He should never have gotten involved, shouldn't have listened to Liz. She encouraged him to intervene, it was her words that strengthened his resolve. And now, because of them, Jen's life was worse than ever. He'd put her in danger.

He sat up straight, set his feet on the ground and stared at the wall. He needed to take a walk. It was dark, but his eyes would adjust soon enough. There had to be something he could do to fix this, but he needed time to think it through. With a glance at his packed suitcase, he pushed out the door and headed down the stairs, anger and frustration propelling each footstep.

𝕤 15 𝕖

Sunscreen gleamed on Liz's skin. She slipped a coverup over her swimsuit. It flowed, white lace and linen over her lightly tanned skin. She picked up a pair of over-sized sunglasses, slipped them onto her face, and regarded herself in the mirror.

There was something missing. She found a long, green pendant necklace—costume jewellery—and slipped it over her head. There. Perfect.

There was a knock on her bedroom door. She hurried to open it, smiling at Ivy and Margot.

"I'm ready to go," she said, ducking back into the room for her beach bag.

She pulled the door shut behind her and hesitated a moment to stare at Rob's door. She hadn't seen him at all that morning although she'd peeped out a few times; and hadn't heard him either, which was unusual. He'd promised to meet her friends, so she wondered what'd happened to him.

"It's the perfect day for a swim at the beach," said Margot, linking one arm through Liz's, the other through Ivy's, as they walked down the wide staircase side by side.

"Breakfast smells amazing," added Ivy, licking her lips.

"Mima's a wonderful cook," replied Liz. "She always puts on a feast."

That morning was no exception. There were pancakes, freshly made waffles, bacon and eggs, and piles of tomatoes, cut in half and grilled in olive oil and oregano, alongside homemade bread, and mounds of freshly cut tropical fruits.

"Mango!" exclaimed Ivy, reaching for a plate. "And look at these peaches, they're so big."

The three women piled their plates high with food and found a table against the window.

"This is amazing. I'm glad I already put on my swimsuit, otherwise I'm not sure I'd be able to squeeze into it after this meal," said Margot with a laugh as she slipped a piece of fresh mango between her lips. Brown curls frizzed around her face, and her hazel eyes sparkled.

Liz chuckled. "I know exactly what you mean."

"So, where's this mystery man of yours?" asked Ivy as she buttered a piece of toast.

"He's not my man," replied Liz with a shake of her head. "And I'm not sure where Rob is. He's usually at breakfast, or in his room, at this time of morning. I knocked on his door earlier, but he wasn't there. I hope everything's okay with his daughter..."

Margot chewed a piece of bacon, swallowed. "What's wrong with his daughter?"

Liz wasn't sure how much she could share with her friends. It was a delicate situation, and she was certain Rob would want her to be discrete. Still, it would help her to talk to her friends about it.

She sighed. "She's having some domestic issues. Her husband... isn't very nice."

Ivy and Margot seemed to read between the lines exactly the way she'd hoped they would.

"Is she leaving him?" asked Margot.

"I'm not sure. I hope so. But perhaps that's where Rob is, with Jen and the kids. I know he was worried about them."

Mima bustled into the room, checking on the buffet, then greeting each of the guests with a smile. She stopped at their table with her lips pulled into a wide grin.

"Good morning, ladies. How are you on this fine morning?"

"We're wonderful, thank you, Mima," replied Liz. "And the food is scrumptious, as always."

"Well, thank you my dear. I'm glad you're enjoying yourselves."

"Mima..." said Margot. "We were outside on the verandah last night and there was a possum..."

Mima laughed. "Oh yes, that would be Cocoa. She's a cheeky one. What did she do? Climb your leg?"

"She stole my apple."

Mima laughed, a big belly laugh that shook her whole body and squeezed her eyes shut tight. "That sounds like Cocoa. She's our resident ring-tailed possum."

Margot chuckled. "That's good to know."

"Well, you ladies enjoy a scandalous day together." Mima winked, then lumbered away.

"So, what's the plan?" asked Ivy, delicately patting her lips with a napkin.

"Shopping!" said Margot.

"I'd love to walk along the beach," added Liz.

Margot rolled her eyes. "More walking..."

"It's good for us."

Margot grunted.

"So, should we go to Coolangatta then? There's a beach and shopping. Plus, I wouldn't mind grabbing a nice coffee somewhere together."

"Sounds like the perfect day," replied Liz with a smile.

THE WAY THE SUN SHONE, GLARING OFF THE TOP OF THE water, gave Coolangatta a bright, bleached look. When she stepped into the sand, shoes swinging in one hand, Liz gasped. It was hot. The soles of her feet burned more with each step. She hurried forward.

Margot came after her. "Ah... Oh... hot!" She shuffled past Liz at a jog.

Liz laughed. Ivy loped by, long legs easily covering ground, toes digging into the stand with each stride.

Finally, they reached the hard-packed sand. The moisture seeped through, soothing Liz's burned feet. She slowed her pace with a sigh.

They lay on the beach, side by side on the sand. Each sprawled on a colourful beach towel. Liz dipped her over-heated body in the ocean a few times and even took a walk along the length of the beach to the end and back again. Then she sat back on her towel, reaching for the latest book, a mystery set in the south of France.

"Oh, look at that," said Margot, sitting up on her towel. Sweat drew a damp line along her forehead. She pointed out to sea.

Liz's gaze followed her gesture. A boat hummed over the water's surface, a bright, billowing parachute hovering in the air above.

"Parasailing," injected Ivy.

"I've always wanted to do that," said Margot, her voice edged with excitement.

Ivy smiled. "I'll do it with you. It looks fun."

They both faced Liz, expectant.

Liz grimaced. "Not me. You two enjoy yourselves. This book is calling my name."

Margot pouted. "You're no fun."

"Yes, I am. I'd simply prefer to read rather than be hurtled through the air above a speed boat."

"They're not hurtling... look they're hanging suspended, gliding gracefully. It looks completely safe, and so much fun." Margot folded her arms and set them on top of bent knees to watch the parasailer.

"No thanks." Liz lowered herself back onto the towel, holding the book open above her face.

"You used to be fun," murmured Margot.

"What?" Liz pushed up onto her elbows.

"I'm just saying... you used to take risks, have adventures... you've gotten..." Margot shrugged. "Anyway. I think we should do it."

"I've gotten what?" Liz's brow furrowed and irritation stirred in her gut.

"Nothing. I shouldn't have said anything. Forget it." Margot's lips formed a thin line.

"No, you were about to say something. Spit it out."

Ivy stood, brushed the sand from her legs.

"Boring. I was going to say you've gotten boring. You don't want to do anything anymore, except hide in that big old house, read books, and take walks."

"I'm not boring." Liz's throat thickened.

"I know you're not... I think you're *acting* boring these days. You're scared, after everything that happened, you've lost your risk-taking mojo." Margot's cheeks flushed red. "Look, I'm sorry, I shouldn't have said anything. Forget it. Ivy and I are going parasailing. We'll see you after."

Liz jumped to her feet. "I'm coming with you. And I'm not boring!" She threw her book down on the towel.

Ivy shook her head silently, a smile tugging at the corners of her mouth. "Come on you two, let's go before a war breaks out."

Liz fell into step beside them as they headed for a big, red tent at the end of the beach. A sign advertised parasailing in bold, white letters.

"Do you really think I'm boring?" asked Liz.

Margot wrapped an arm around her shoulders, squeezing her from one side. "No, of course I don't. Sometimes I don't think before I speak."

"No kidding," piped up Ivy.

Margot huffed.

"I haven't been doing as much in the last few years because I've been feeling a bit low. That's all. Besides, we're all getting older... isn't that normal, to slow things down a bit?"

"We're not that old, and you're younger than Ivy and me," replied Margot with a wrinkled nose.

"Not dead yet," laughed Ivy.

"So, you both think I should take more risks?" asked Liz. She couldn't believe her friends thought she was boring. After all their years together, all the adventures they'd had. She hadn't realised they felt that way.

"It wouldn't hurt," replied Ivy. "Although, I don't think you're boring, I think you're licking your wounds. And everyone needs time to do that."

"True, but you can't stay in that place forever," replied Margot.

They waited in line for their turn behind the boat. Ivy went first, and Liz could hear her squeals from where she stood as the boat roared away then came back again, Ivy sailing in the air behind it.

It was her turn next. Nerves squirmed in her stomach. She waited while the attendant strapped her in and gave her instructions, the nervousness spreading throughout her body in waves, heart thudding.

What was she doing? This was crazy? She could get hurt

or drown in the ocean with a big colourful parachute sucking her into the water as it fell around her.

She faced Margot and Ivy, her eyes wide, fear stealing her voice. Both women grinned. Margot gave her a thumbs up.

Liz inhaled a long, slow breath.

Calm down. Everything's going to be fine. Deep breaths. I'm not going to die today.

It amazed her how quickly and easily she was propelled into the air from the back of the boat. She held on tight with her hands, clutching at the harness, her knuckles white. Then slowly, her grasp loosened, and she looked around, taking in the blue green waters, the golden beach, the shrinking figures of people rushing the waves, lying on the sand, or strolling hand in hand.

A laugh bubbled up within her.

"Woohoo!" she shouted.

Adrenaline lit up every nerve in her body. She craned her neck to look behind, then forward again. It was beautiful from where she hung. Perspective made everything smaller. Nothing looked out of control, nothing scary, or headed for disaster. Everything seemed ordered, simple, safe.

She knew it was illusion. Safety didn't exist. Not absolutely. But from where she sat, she finally felt it. The irony pushed a smile onto her face. She was suspended in the air being pulled along by a boat, and yet she felt safe for the first time in years. Safe, strong, and independent. As though she could do anything, didn't need anyone else to do it with her. She could do it alone if she wanted. She was capable, in charge of her own destiny.

She yelled again, the sound releasing something primal within her. It swelled and pulled from her throat, taking a sob with it. Shouted again. This time, it was a victory cry, and she yelled until her throat was raw.

When she made it back to Ivy and Margot her voice was hoarse, but a grin hung on her face and wouldn't fade.

"Did you have fun?" asked Ivy.

She nodded. "It was great."

Something had lifted inside of her, had released her from its grasp. She felt free, happy. She didn't hang her head with her usual shame, she held it high. She could do this. She could face life on her own. She'd been rejected but she would recover. Hope glimmered on the horizon.

Next it was Margot's turn and she was whooping before she even made it to the boat. She sailed quietly then returned to them with a pained look on her face, brows furrowed over dark eyes.

When she reached the sand, she hobbled towards them.

"What's wrong?" Ivy and Liz hurried to help her, each looping an arm around her frame.

She leaned on them for support as she winced her way up the beach. "I twisted my ankle on the boat."

"Oh no," replied Liz

They helped her back to their towels, and she sat down with a grimace. She examined her ankle.

Liz sat beside her, peering at the injured limb. "I think it's swelling."

"Definitely," agreed Ivy.

"Great," added Margot with a sigh.

"So much for risk-taking," said Liz, her eyes sparkling.

Margot laughed. "I deserved that."

"I think we should take you to the emergency room, just in case," said Ivy.

"What? No, I'm sure it will be fine." Margot shook her head. "That would spoil the entire day."

"Come on, it's better to find out for sure if it's broken or sprained. It's swelling up like a puffer fish."

Margot groaned. "But, our beach day..."

"Maybe we'll still have time to shop later," suggested Liz.

"Ugh, I can't believe this."

Liz and Ivy helped Margot reach the road, all their things swinging from their arms in beach bags. They hailed a cab from there and made it to the Emergency Room in fifteen minutes. When they got there, they gave the nurse Margot's details, then settled into the hard, plastic chairs in the waiting area.

"This could be a long wait," grumbled Margot.

"It's fine," said Liz, patting Margot's leg. "At least we all brought books."

Ivy pulled reading glasses from her bag, pushing them onto her nose with a laugh. "I guess this is how adventuring looks in your fifties."

Liz huffed. "Something to look forward to."

"How long until you're fifty?" asked Margot. "Three years?"

Liz nodded. "Three years." It felt strange to say that. Only three years until she turned fifty. She'd well and truly stumbled into middle age. Still, it felt as though she'd been young only yesterday. Time had passed so quickly it made her head spin.

It took three hours before Margot was officially found to have sprained her ankle. She hadn't broken anything, but had torn a ligament, so they bandaged it up and gave her crutches for walking. When the three of them finally emerged from the hospital, the bright sunlight made Liz blink.

"Now what?" she asked.

"Shopping?" suggested Ivy. "Do you think you can manage, Margot?"

Margot gave a determined nod. "Let's do it."

They found a new shopping centre with plenty of boutique shops to satisfy all three different tastes and styles. After an hour of shopping, they stopped for a coffee, then shopped some more. Liz bought herself a new swimsuit, navy with silver stripes. She also purchased a lacy coverall in pink that flowed nicely around her legs and gave her shoulders some protection from the sun without feeling stifling.

Finally, they were ready to eat tea. They headed across the street to Jack Evan's Boat Harbour, on the advice of a local, and found a small fish and chip shop perched on the edge of the harbour. They bought enough for three, found a picnic table and sat with the food between the three of them, eating with their fingers and watching as pelicans and seagulls soared, dipped, and called around the water's edge.

Boats were moored on one side of the harbour: yachts with their tall spires waving gently as the water lapped at their hulls, and small tin fishing boats. The sun drew long shadows across the sand as it set behind them. Finally, the heat of the day dissipated, and a cool breeze lifted the damp hair from the back of Liz's neck.

When they reached the inn, it was dark. There were a few guests in the living room, but otherwise the building was quiet. Liz wished her friends good night. It'd been a wonderful day, and she was looking forward to a cool shower and to slipping under her covers to sleep. She was exhausted.

She hesitated outside Rob's room. Where was he? She hadn't seen him all day. Had he checked out already without telling her? Surely, he wouldn't do that. Perhaps he was simply giving her space to spend time with her friends, though she found she missed his company and missed his smiling face.

She stepped to the door, raised a hand, and knocked gently. There was no response. She tried again, louder this time. He didn't answer. Her brow furrowed. She hoped nothing was wrong.

With a sigh, she returned to her door, went inside, shut it behind her, and leaned on it a moment, then headed for the bathroom. She'd have to try his door again in the morning. If he still didn't answer, she could ask Bindi about it. Maybe the inn's manager would know where he was and if he was okay. She undressed quickly and stepped beneath the steady stream of water, letting it rinse off the sweat, sea water and sunscreen. The gentle pummelling soothed her reddened skin and tired eyes.

Before long she was fast asleep in bed, dreaming of flying through the air and landing against a firm chest. When she looked up, she saw Rob's face, his eyes burning with desire. She lifted a hand to caress his face and he turned into a possum who ducked beneath her palm and scurried up a tree branch to sit out of reach and watch her with glowing eyes. She woke with a start, eyes flinging wide open, heart thundering.

With a sigh, she rolled onto her side and stared at the wall. She was worried about Rob. The last time she'd heard from him, he was encouraging Jen to leave her husband. Maybe things had progressed, or perhaps gotten worse. She wished she knew. She should have tried to find him that morning before they left for the beach. She tossed and turned for another hour before she fell to sleep again and this time her slumber was dreamless.

❦ 16 ❦

28TH DECEMBER 1996

CABARITA BEACH

Rob pushed the cereal around his bowl with a spoon. He stared into the milk, his appetite lagging. He hadn't been able to face a plate of pancakes, though they smelled divine. Instead, had opted for Weetbix with slices of banana and honey drizzled over the top. Still, he'd only had a few bites and couldn't seem to bring himself to eat more. A few Christmas decorations still hung on the walls, but most had been removed. The inn seemed empty without them.

His stomach churned.

He'd been calling Jen ever since their last hushed phone conversation, but she hadn't picked up. No one had. It was as if they'd disappeared. He'd swung by their house the day before, no one was home. He didn't know what to do now.

Should he report them missing? But what if they weren't missing, and he only further angered Neil.

Maybe he was exaggerating things in his head, making them more dramatic than they actually were. Surely Neil wouldn't hurt his family? He was grumpy and had anger issues, that was true, but he wouldn't take things further. Would he?

Jen's whispered words kept ringing in his ears.

"...It was bad...."

What did that mean? How bad? He needed answers and wouldn't find them in the bottom of his cereal bowl. Anger turned his stomach.

"I'm stuck, this is my life..."

He shook his head. That she believed it was clear enough, but he couldn't believe it himself. No one was ever stuck. There was always another way, a way out. No matter what the circumstances.

He glanced up as Liz and two other women waltzed into the breakfast nook. They were chattering and laughing. One of the women leaned on a pair of crutches.

Liz caught his eye and ushered the others to where he sat.

"Rob, there you are. I've been looking for you. I want to introduce my friends to you—this is Margot..." she gestured towards the woman on the crutches, her hazel eyes gleamed as she shook Rob's outstretched hand.

"...And this is Ivy." She indicated a tall, lithe woman with shining blonde hair and wide blue eyes. He shook her hand as well.

"Pleased to meet you both," he said. Though he couldn't muster much more than a few polite words after that.

They chatted for a while, then found a table close by. He sighed with relief and returned his attention to his cereal. He didn't have the energy to deal with social niceties, his entire focus was on his family. He had to help Jen out of this situation. It was all he could think about. Especially since he was the one who'd escalated the issue and possibly put them all in danger.

He watched the news. He knew how these things could go if they weren't careful about how they handled it.

Liz tapped him on the shoulder, and he spun to face her with a frown.

"Everything okay?" she asked, her smile tentative.

He shook his head, stood to his feet, and guided her out of the breakfast nook, one hand touching her elbow.

"What is it? What's wrong?" she asked.

He stopped, faced her, and ran his fingers through his hair. How did he say this? Anger and fear muddied his thoughts.

"Everything's worse."

Her brows knitted together. "What do you mean? With Jen?"

"Yes." Irritation buzzed in his gut. "Yes, with Jen. I should've stayed out of it. But now, I've made it all worse. Jen's a virtual prisoner in her home and there's nothing I can do about it."

She pressed both hands to her mouth. Eyes wide. "Oh, I'm sorry, Rob."

He grunted. "I don't know what to do. Should I call the police? Go over there and camp out until they come home? Stay away and hope things get better? I don't know... I feel so helpless. She's my baby; I used to be able to protect her. Pick her up and set her on my knee if she was hurt, with a kiss to make it better. Now, I can't do anything but offer her a few words of encouragement."

Liz nodded. "I know. Parenting gets harder, I think. Letting go of our control is the hardest part of all. But Jen's in charge of her own choices..."

"And what choice does she have? That man is dominating

her and won't let her make a choice." Anger tinged his words, and he pressed his hands to his hips.

Liz didn't respond.

He shook his head. "I'm glad your friends are here. Tell them I'm sorry I wasn't friendlier; I'm not really feeling like myself."

She smiled. "I'll tell them. And you take care of yourself. Getting worked up over this won't help things. You need a clear head if you're going to make the best decision about what to do."

He sighed. She was right. He dipped his head. "I know. You're right. I wish I knew..."

"You'll make the right choice."

He inhaled a sharp breath. "I'll see you later."

She nodded.

He walked away, feeling her eyes on his back. He shouldn't have snapped at her. She'd encouraged him, supported him, and he'd reacted like an old grouch. If she never spoke to him again, he wouldn't blame her.

He'd been foolish to imagine a future for him and Liz. It'd been fleeting, a momentary dream. But he could see now that it could never work between them. He'd push her away, or she'd lock him out. The two of them had too much baggage to make a real go of it. Besides, he had his life organised, structured. And he was doing just fine on his own.

* * *

HE COULDN'T THINK WHAT ELSE TO DO OTHER THAN GET IN his car and go for a drive. Rob set off in the direction of Jen's house, then changed his mind and stopped in Kingscliff instead. He parked beneath a large conifer tree, donned a hat, then climbed out, and shoved his hands deep into the pockets of his shorts before aiming for the beach.

He passed a small kids' playground. Children laughed and squealed as they rode a roundabout once painted in bright colours, but now chipped by use and made pale by the sun. Others slid down a gleaming metal slide, then ran off holding onto the backs of their legs. The sun beat down on everything making it scalding hot. Waves of heat emanated from the slide and the sand that filled the playground.

On the beach, he strode with purpose, arms pumping by his sides. Exercise always helped him to think things through. Usually, after a good walk, he knew what to do, or at least felt better about it. But this walk wasn't helping. Every step he took filled him with more helplessness and anger, and every swooping gull stole his hope.

It was easier to deal with loss or pain in his own life than to see his child enduring it and be unable to do anything about it.

Finally, he slumped onto the sand and rested his arms on bent knees to watch the waves as they collapsed against the shore. Sweat made a damp patch on his shirt down the middle of his back. It trickled beneath his arms and down both sides of his face.

A family caught his attention. There were three children, varying ages. The youngest looked to be about two years old, not much younger than Daniel was. He watched as the grandparents swung the two-year old high in the air between them, each holding onto one chubby hand. His delighted squeals filled the air, echoing over the noise of the waves.

An ache filled his heart.

That's how it should be. He and Martha, swinging little Daniel between them. Their family laughing and chattering around them. Happy, safe, brimming with love.

Instead, he was here alone, staring into the waves. Clouds gathered overhead, bulging with rain. The breeze picked up, humid with gusts that carried sand in their grasp and pelted the tiny grains against his bare legs.

The parents knelt in the sand to help one of the children build a sandcastle. The grandparents joined in, then the grandmother wandered off with the eldest child to draw pictures in the wet sand with their toes.

The youngest child helped the building project for a while. Then he too meandered away, but in the opposite direction. He found a few shells that he pushed unceremoniously into his shirt pocket. Then, he ran at the water's edge. A wave, already spent, rushed at him and he turned with a laugh to hurry from its reach, little legs pumping.

He stumbled, fell in the sand, and picked himself up. He was getting too close the water and the waves had grown rough as the storm built overhead.

Rob glanced back at the family. Surely someone would call out to the boy, urge him to return to the sandcastle. But no one looked up, no one seemed to notice how far from the group he was straying.

The boy fell again, this time the wave enveloped him in an instant, then dragged him into its arms, pulling the boy tumbling back into the ocean with it.

Rob jumped to his feet and ran to the boy. Still, the family hadn't noticed. The boy didn't make a sound. At least none that rose above the noise of the ocean as it beat on the shoreline.

"Hey!" called Rob, jumping over the first small wave. "Hey!"

The parents looked up, curiosity etching their faces. Then, the mother glanced around. She stood to her feet.

"Chris? Chris? Where's Chris?"

Her voice was snatched away by the wind in his ears. Rob was focused on the bobbing head, a few metres ahead of him. He couldn't lose sight of the boy, the next wave might whisk him away, losing him in the ocean's swirling, frothing bosom.

"Chris!" the parents were behind him now, headed in the same direction as he was. But they wouldn't reach the boy, not in time.

Rob dove into an oncoming wave, the cold water hitting him with a force that had him gasping for air when he emerged. He shook the droplets from his hair, plunged again.

This time, his hands closed around the boy. He grasped hold of the child's shirt and lifted him with a grunt to the water's surface. Another wave, and this one landed on top of them both. He pushed up through it, keeping the boy's head higher than his own.

The boy's eyes were open, wide, and searching. His mouth opened then, sputtering, coughing, and wailing.

Relief coursed through Rob's veins. He laughed, pulled the boy to his chest as he trudged to the sandy shore.

"You're okay. You're fine, everything's okay now. You got a bit wet there, didn't you?" He murmured in the boy's ear.

Halfway back to shore the boy's father reached him, nostrils flared.

"Chris!" he called.

The boy reached for him. Rob handed him over with a smile. "He's fine."

"Thank you," replied the man, enveloping the boy with both arms and heading for dry land.

The boy's family fussed over him, checking every part of him to make sure he wasn't hurt. Then, they each turned to Rob. They thanked him, embraced him. The mother cried in his arms; the father shook his hand twice.

Both grandparents stood nearby, in shock, shushing the other children and holding them as they watched with wide eyes.

They invited Rob to eat with him, but he thanked them

for the offer and returned to his car, then he sat in the front seat, clenching the steering wheel.

He felt alive. His blood whizzed through his veins, still carrying adrenaline on its back. He breathed deeply, smiling at the horizon. He'd saved the boy's life. No one else was watching, and if he hadn't been there, he'd have heard the news on the local station that night and felt a strange sadness over it. But he'd been there. The exhilaration of it filled him with a joy he couldn't explain.

Maybe he couldn't save his only family, but he'd saved Chris. The boy's name replayed over and over in his thoughts, the mother's voice carrying it thin on a rising wind.

That was what mattered. Love. Helping someone. Saving those that could be saved. The connections made between strangers who would step in and help one another.

He wasn't alone in the world. Sometimes it felt that way, but there were people all around him. People who would step in if he needed help the way he'd done for Chris.

Family connections mattered most. He'd do anything to help his family and the ones he loved. Life was fleeting, there weren't many chances for happiness. He'd pushed Liz away, made things worse for Jen. But he could fix it. Could make things better. He couldn't give up on himself yet, or on them.

🎄 17 🎄

29TH DECEMBER 1996

CABARITA BEACH

The inn was quieter than it had been for days. Liz stopped at the bottom of the stairs to look around. Where was everyone? She'd slept late, then stayed in bed, thinking about everything that'd happened. Her encounter with Rob weighed heavily on her thoughts.

Her heart ached for him and what his family was going through. There was no easy solution, no final answer or platitude she could share with him to make things easier. She wished she could help ease his pain, but she couldn't.

She peered at the Christmas tree, lights still glowing softly in the daylight. Had Christmas really only been a few days ago? It seemed like a lifetime. She'd dreaded spending the holiday alone, but it'd passed as it always did, the world moving on again at the same steady pace. The back door creaked open, and Ivy poked her head through the opening.

"Come on, Liz. We're having breakfast outside under the gum trees." She smiled as she beckoned with one hand.

It was their last day together at the inn. Margot and Ivy were leaving, headed to the airport after breakfast. They'd already packed, and their suitcases stood by the reception counter. Liz wasn't headed home until the next day. She had one more night at the inn, and she was beginning to regret that decision. She wanted to leave with Ivy and Margot. They could've caught the same flight, shared a drink at the airport bar and a few more laughs. Still, it would give her a chance to say goodbye to Rob, something she found herself dreading more with each passing day.

They hadn't spent much time together since her friends arrived at the Waratah, but before that, they'd connected in a way she hadn't experienced with any man since her ex-husband. And, even then, she'd been so young, it'd been more about attraction than about connection. Rob was the kind of man she could imagine growing old with, and the realisation shocked her like a bolt of electricity to her heart. She had to talk to him, to resolve things between them before she left.

She wandered outside and found her friends seated at a long table with other guests. Covered in a white tablecloth, the trestle table was filled with good things to eat. Waffles, pancakes, bacon, bowls of scrambled eggs, jugs of orange juice —her mouth watered at the sight of it. The scent tickled her nostrils and she licked her lips, suddenly aware of her hunger.

She sat between Margot and Ivy. Margot's crutches were leaned up against the trunk of one of the nearest trees.

"I'm so glad the two of you came to see me," she said, reaching for a bowl of scrambled eggs and spooning some onto her plate.

Soft music emanated from within the inn, magpies played a melody over it, warbles filling the still, morning air with song. The sun hovered, lifting from the earth to smother the cooler night air with its heat. Beneath the trees, the breakfast table carried its impressive display of food dappled by moving light filtering through the leaves above.

"I'm glad too," replied Margot. She gulped a mouthful of juice. "Even with the sprained ankle, it's definitely been more fun than staying home. I'd probably have cleaned my house and run errands; I can't help myself when I'm there. It's good to get away and find some rest. It'll be back to work soon enough."

Ivy nodded, still chewing on a piece of bacon. She swallowed. "I love you guys, we're a pretty good team, aren't we?"

Liz's throat tightened. She'd see her friends again soon, but it felt like something was ending. This trip had been a turning point for her, a line in the sand. She wasn't going home as the same closed off, shame-filled woman she'd been. She was confident, hopeful of a future she could build on her own. Her friends were a big part of that transformation.

"I wanted to thank both of you," she said, reaching for their hands and squeezing them with her own. "This holiday has helped me to see that things in my life have to change. And that I can change them myself. That I don't have to hide away or wallow, but I can decide what I want my future to look like and go after it. And I couldn't have figured all of that out without you. You're my best friends, and I'm so glad I have you in my life." Tears tickled the corners of her eyes. She blinked them away.

Margot leaned over to kiss her cheek. "That's what we're here for. Besides, you've done the same for me plenty of times over the years." Her voice was thick with emotion.

Ivy wrapped Liz in an embrace. "I'm always here; whenever you need me."

Liz nodded. "I wish you didn't have to leave until tomorrow. What am I going to do without you?"

Margot winked. "Find Rob, maybe have one last date. If you know what I mean."

Liz rolled her eyes. "I always know what you mean. And I really don't think that's going to happen. He's pretty distracted, and he's definitely been pulling away from me. I've hardly seen him since you arrived. I wish he'd talk to me..." She sighed. "But I suppose it doesn't really matter since I'm leaving tomorrow anyway."

Ivy piled fresh slices of mango and peaches onto her plate. She picked one up and chewed thoughtfully. "You know, it isn't every day you find someone you really like. Someone attractive, intelligent, caring... they don't come along often. Definitely not at our age. Most of the good ones are married."

Liz pursed her lips. Ivy wasn't wrong about that. She hadn't been looking for a relationship but had noticed over the past two years that she hadn't met a man she'd connected with once. She'd thought she never would again.

"So, what are you saying?" she asked.

Ivy shrugged. "I think it's worth considering... I don't know, talking to him about what's going on. Don't walk away until you're sure. Do you really think another Rob is going to come along anytime soon?"

Liz shook her head. "No, I can't imagine it. He's... kind of perfect, even if he is completely distracted by his family right now. That's attractive too. I admire how passionate he is about taking care of the people he loves."

"Sounds like you have some things to discuss with the handsome Rob," added Margot with a grin.

After breakfast they said their goodbyes. Liz embraced each of her friends, whispered a thanks in their ear, then slumped into an armchair as she listened to the sounds of their cab pulling out of the inn's driveway. Then silence fell. Only the chirp of birds and a few clangs and bangs in the kitchen. She wandered in there and found Mima wiping the benches with a cloth.

Mima smiled. "And then there was one…"

Liz chuckled. "Yep. They're gone and I'll be following tomorrow."

Footsteps fell behind her. "Good morning everyone." Rob's voice was gentle, full.

He smiled. His eyes met hers for a moment, seeming to look into her soul. "Good morning, Liz."

She nodded. "Good morning, Rob. I hope you slept well."

"I did. Thanks."

"Would anyone like a cup of tea?" asked Mima, flicking on the jug to boil.

"I'd love one," replied Liz. She took a seat at the kitchen table.

Rob joined her, sliding into the chair next to her. "Yes please."

White-shirted staff popped in and out of the kitchen, unpacking and putting away the breakfast things from outside. One young man stayed behind to stack dishes in the dishwasher.

While Mima busied herself getting the tea ready, Liz leaned closer to Rob. "You seem more chipper this morning."

He shrugged. "As you said, Jen's an adult and she has to make her own choices. It's not up to me to take care of her anymore. Of course, I hope she does what's best for her and the children, but I can't control that, and spending my time worrying about it won't help."

Liz smiled. "Good for you."

"Look I'm sorry I was a grouch yesterday…" His brow furrowed, and he rested a gentle, warm hand on her arm.

She inhaled a quick breath. "It's fine. You've had a lot on your mind." His hand remained on her arm, and she liked the way it felt.

"Home tomorrow?" he asked, leaning back in his chair.

She nodded. "You?"

He chuckled. "Back to the grindstone... well, after the New Year anyway. I can't believe how fast the time flew by."

"Are you glad you came?" she asked.

He nodded. "I think so. Although I would've liked to see more of the kids. Still, I'll take what I can get. And it's more time than I've had with them in a while."

"They're great kids. You're very blessed."

Mima set two mugs of tea in front of them, then went back for her own. She lowered herself into a chair with a grunt.

"Another Christmas over," she said, then sipped the tea.

Liz cupped her hands around her mug. "Do you like Christmas, Mima?"

Mima nodded, a smile crept across her lips. "I love Christmas. One year, back when Edie and Paul owned the place, she was my best friend who passed recently..."

"I'm so sorry Mima," interrupted Liz.

Mima nodded. "Thank you, love... well this one Christmas, she and Paul had decided they'd get the guests involved. Edie loved to play games, to decorate, and she loved her guests. So, her plan was to have the guests help decorate the inn for Christmas. She was so excited, she thought everyone would be as enthralled by the concept as she was. But I tell you what, there was tinsel as far as the eye could see..." Mima chuckled, her eyes focused on something far away. "Decorations in every colour. Nothing matched. But Edie was over the moon about it all. There were candles, ornaments, sprigs of wildflowers, twinkle lights... so many decorations covering every surface of the place, it was like a sparkly assault on the eyes." Mima laughed. "Well, one of the guests put a lit candle right under a strand of tinsel, and before we knew it, the sitting room was on fire."

"Oh no," exclaimed Liz.

Rob's eyebrows arched.

"Yes indeed, we could have lost the whole inn that Christmas. Thankfully, Paul had the sense to run for the fire extinguisher and put out the fire before it spread. We ended up with a white Christmas tree, and a burned wall... and that was the end of the guests' involvement in decorating for the holidays."

Liz laughed and Rob did too. She caught him looking at her and a flush crept over her cheeks. He didn't break away, their gaze connected for several long moments.

"What about you, Liz? Any Christmas stories spring to mind?"

Liz took a sip of tea as she searched through memories. "We've definitely had a few interesting holidays over the years. One Christmas, Cam and I took the kids to Port Macquarie to visit my parents. They lived there for a few years before moving to Cairns. We opened gifts around their small, plastic tree in the morning, then we decided to go to the beach. The kids had gotten a beach ball and some sand toys as gifts, and they wanted to try them out.

"So, we all wandered down the trail by the house to the nearest beach in our swimsuits, with towels and a change of clothes in a bag that I'd slung over my shoulder. We had a lovely time, the water was perfect, the waves were small, and the kids enjoyed their new toys. After I'd had a good, long swim, I decided to change out of my wet swimsuit. I went to the public toilets, slipped out of my suit and changed into a lovely new outfit I'd bought for the occasion.

"When I stepped out of the toilets to rejoin the family, a magpie swooped me. Its beak tapped my head and gave me a fright. I was running for my life with my hands waving over my head. I shouted at Cam, and he watched me run towards him with a confused look on his face just as I tripped over a tree root and landed flat in a mud puddle right in front of a crowd of people. The family teased me for years about the Christmas I walked home from the beach covered head to toe in mud because of a killer bird."

Mima and Rob both chuckled over that. Liz laughed along with them.

"I hope you weren't hurt," said Rob.

"No, only my pride."

Mima gulped the last of her tea. "That was a good one, Liz. Unfortunately, I have to get going. There's a lot to do today, and I'm feeling a bit worse for wear."

"You should try to get some rest," said Liz, her brows drawing together.

"You're right. I do believe this Christmas has worn me out completely."

"Why don't you go home?" suggested Rob. "I'm sure the staff can manage without you."

Mima's lips pursed. "It is only the two of you here today."

"Just us?" asked Liz, her eyebrows quirked.

"Just you two tonight," confirmed Mima. "In fact, if you don't mind, I might let you fend for yourself in the kitchen tonight. Maybe I will go home and put my feet up."

"Definitely. We can manage without you." Liz patted Mima's arm. "You have to take care of yourself."

Mima nodded, stood to her feet with a groan. "That's it then. You're on your own tonight." She winked. "Don't get up to too much mischief without me."

Liz chuckled. "I'm not really the mischief-making type."

"Oh, I wouldn't be too sure about that. Anyone can make mischief given the right set of circumstances. And not all mischief is bad. You should always try to get up to a little mischief, at least that's been my life's motto." Mima laughed.

When Mima left, the kitchen was quiet again. The staff had mostly finished cleaning up the breakfast things and were struggling to carry the pieces of the table over the lawn to the garage. Liz could see them through the windows that faced the back yard.

She sipped her tea in the momentary silence.

"So, it's only you and me tonight..." said Rob.

Liz nodded with a smile. "I guess so."

"Scrabble?" he asked.

She laughed. "Sounds good."

"I'm glad we'll get to spend our last night here together," he replied.

Her heart skipped a beat.

"Me too."

"Want to go for a swim?" he asked.

She nodded. "That would be perfect. I'll go and get changed."

She drained the last of her cup and hurried upstairs to change into her swimsuit. She'd miss this place when she left it. Something she'd never have thought possible a week earlier. She'd even miss the mischievous possum she'd seen perched on a tree branch or trundling along the verandah rail in the dim light of dusk a few times since it stole Margot's apple. And she'd miss Mima, Bindi, and Rob. One last night with Rob, and then it was back home to start her life over. The thought stirred nerves in her gut.

❧ 18 ❧

A tapping sound on the window woke Liz from her nap. She blinked a few times, pried her eyes open, and rolled onto her side with a sigh. It was hard to adjust her senses for a few moments—time, location. Her eyes focused on the bedside clock. It was five p.m. Had she really slept for three hours?

She slid her feet to the floor, shaking the sleep from her eyes with a wide yawn. The tapping sound caught her ear again and she wandered to the window to investigate. A tree branch reached toward the window, and one end of a small shoot scraped against the glass in the breeze. She peered skyward—dark clouds gathered overhead.

Her goal for the afternoon had been a last walk along the beach. Perhaps she still had time before the storm hit. It wouldn't matter too much if she got a little wet, she often enjoyed walking in the rain in summer. It was refreshing, and not far to go for a hot shower and a change of clothes.

She yawned again, changed into a pair of bike shorts and an oversized t-shirt, then headed downstairs, her ponytail bobbing with each step she took.

The inn was quiet and a little dark. Before she stepped outside, she flicked on the kitchen light. Where was everyone? Mima had mentioned she wouldn't be around this evening, but she couldn't see any of the other staff either. Bindi might have been hiding in the office behind the kitchen, or perhaps in one of the rooms upstairs. That still didn't explain the complete silence downstairs.

With a shrug, she headed out the back door and along the winding path that would take her to the small cove. She smiled at the sight of the rolling waves, the seagulls floating, hovering, and alighting on the beach, the black rocky outcroppings with white sea spray showering over them.

She smiled and strode along the sandy shore, the cool breeze blowing the oppressive heat of the day away and inland. A drop of water spat at her forehead and she wiped it away with a frown. She could turn back now but preferred to keep going for as long as she could.

In the end she managed to walk for twenty minutes before turning around. The clouds had dropped a few small spits of rain on her head, but nothing more. Still, she knew it would only be a matter of time. The cloud cover had filled every available piece of blue in the sky and swirled darkly with an impressive yet threatening depth of colours—every shade of dark blue, grey, and black.

Thunder rumbled in the distance, then again closer. She picked up the pace, hurrying along the wet sand, then cutting across the dry towards the inn, its roof jutting over the tops of the trees ahead.

By the time she reached the back door, fat drops of rain left dark spots on the edge of the verandah. She pushed inside, breathing hard, and slumped into a seat at the kitchen table.

When her breathing slowed, she looked around, listening for any noise. Still nothing. She frowned. It was strange to be in the inn surrounded by quiet. There was usually plenty of noise, the sound of a vacuum whirring, the bang of pots and pans in the kitchen, the murmur of conversation or the hum of the television set in the sitting room.

She grabbed a glass of water from the tap, rinsed the glass, and set it on the sink then explored the ground floor, looking for signs of life. She found Rob in the sitting room, reading a thick book. He glanced up at her over the rims of his glasses as she wandered in.

"There you are," he said. "I thought I'd been completely abandoned."

She chuckled. "So, did I. I'm relieved to see you, actually. Where is everyone else?"

He shrugged. "I don't know. Mima isn't coming in, and since it's only the two of us tonight I heard one of the staff earlier saying they hadn't been rostered on. I don't have any idea where Bindi is."

"I think we've been forgotten," replied Liz, one eyebrow quirked.

He laughed. "You might be right. I suppose we can survive here for one night on our own. Do you have plans for tea?"

She shook her head. "No plans. Although there's a doozy of a storm headed our way, so I thought I might stay in and try to find something edible in the fridge."

"I'm not particularly hungry, a sandwich would do me fine."

Liz eyed the Christmas tree, its twinkle lights glowing bright in the dimming light. A box sat beside the tree, its top folded open. A few of the ornaments were missing. She went to take a closer look. Someone had begun to put the decorations away in the box, wrapping each ornament in a square of tissue paper. The box beckoned, and she found it difficult to resist. She'd spent too many years organising, putting away, cleaning, tidying, and folding for her to stand beside a half-done tree.

She reached for an ornament—a wooden nutcracker doll with a bright red soldier's uniform—and tugged it from the branch. Then, she took a square of tissue and folded the paper around the doll, tucking the finished product neatly into a corner of the box.

"Want some help?" asked Rob.

She chuckled. "I can't seem to resist the urge to tidy, even when it's not my tree. It's a sickness I'm afraid. I hate to pull you away from your book."

His nose wrinkled. "I'm not enjoying it. Too dark for me. I should've gone for something lighter to read with the mood I'm in." He tucked a bookmark between the pages and rose to join her.

They sat side by side, legs crossed, taking down the decorations around the base of the tree first. Before long, they had a rhythm. They chatted about life, family, and dashed dreams, about hope, the future and clean slates. Liz was surprised to find how much they had in common, how many experiences they shared along with their outlook for the years to come.

She relaxed in his presence. A sense of calm washed over her as she laughed at his stories, offered sympathy over losses, and joined in commiserating over the aches and pains of middle age. Not that he looked middle-aged, though he assured her he was older than she was. She objected he looked younger, but he rightly pointed out that he was in fact a grandfather, when she was not. She couldn't refute the argument.

Still, he didn't look like she'd expect a grandfather to look. He was strong, lithe, with only a smattering of grey hair mixed with the sandy blond. His brown eyes had a few laugh lines, it was true, but then again, so did hers.

"You must have been a teenaged father," she quipped.

He chortled. "Hardly, but we were very young I suppose. It didn't feel too young at the time, but now when I see twenty-three-year-old kids, and how young they are, I can't believe we managed to raise a child at that age."

"It's very young but wasn't unusual at the time."

"Not at all. We were poor as church mice, but we were happy. It was a wonderful time." He sighed, reaching for another ornament.

Liz shifted onto her knees to reach higher up the tree. "I know what you mean. Sometimes, I think things in my life grew worse the more money and success we accumulated. When I remember the happiest times, those were the years we had nothing, lived in a tiny apartment together, and ate a lot of rice for tea."

He laughed. "Exactly. When things were simple."

"Then everything got more complicated, stressful. By the end, we barely had time for each other. Work was going so well, and I was thrilled about what we'd built, but we sacrificed our relationship and family time for it. I wish... well, I wish I'd done so many things differently."

"But the past is the one thing we can't do differently," Rob pointed out with a half-smile playing on his lips. "Much as we'd like to have the chance. I'm not sure we'd do any better given another go-around anyway."

She shrugged. "You're probably right. Although I hope I've learned from my mistakes so that I wouldn't make them again."

"Ditto," he replied.

Just then, a giant crack of thunder shook the inn. It startled Liz and she fell onto her rear with a gasp. "Wow, that one was close."

Rob laughed, wild-eyed. "Yes, it was."

Another boom filled the air, then rain fell hard and loud on the inn's tin roof. It drowned out the sound of their voices.

"We should make sure the windows are shut!" shouted Liz above the din.

Rob nodded and they hurried around the inn, pulling shut all the windows and doors they found open. There were only a few, since the air-conditioning had been functioning all day.

Liz made her way back to the Christmas tree. The lights in the sitting room flickered, then fell dark. The Christmas tree lights did the same. Thunder shook the building again, making Liz's heart thud against her rib cage.

Rob joined her in the sitting room. "Electricity's off," he said.

She nodded. "So, it seems. I wonder if there are candles..."

"Let's look in the kitchen," he suggested.

"I still can't believe they forgot about us and left us completely to our own devices," mumbled Liz, following Rob to the kitchen.

"I agree. I mean, I can understand them overlooking me, but you're completely unforgettable," he said. He winked at her over his shoulder.

She laughed. "I feel like a should have a cymbal to hit after a line like that."

He threw his head back to let out a guffaw, then met her gaze and held it. "You make me laugh, Elizabeth Cranwell. And let me tell you, that is a rare and precious thing."

She watched as he tugged out drawers and searched through cupboards, her heart swelling. He was right, it was a rare and precious thing to find someone you could laugh with.

The thunder seemed to have moved on, its booms decreasing in ferocity as the rain settled in. Liz joined Rob in his search, and before long they'd discovered several candles and a lighter between them.

They set the candles in a dish in the centre of the kitchen table. Liz lit them, then sat to stare into the dancing flames. The room seemed suddenly darker with the light testing its strength. She shivered and leaned towards the candles.

"What is it about fire that's so comforting?" she mused.

He shook his head. "I don't know, but it's definitely one of those things we all share—staring into flames can pass an awful lot of time. It's like watching the waves crash to shore. Something about nature. Both mesmerising and calming all at once."

Liz's stomach gave a loud grumble.

Rob laughed. "Hungry?"

"Starving," she admitted. She jumped to her feet. "Let's see what we can find to eat around here."

They rummaged through the refrigerator and cupboards and ended up with an assortment of items to eat. There was a cheese platter, with double cream brie, camembert, and blue vein cheese, along with Kalamata olives, hummus, and several different types of crackers. Sliced mango, peaches, and nectarines with a handful of fresh cherries left over from breakfast. And fresh bread, bacon, and sun reddened tomatoes with fresh lettuce, which Liz deftly turned into sandwiches with mayonnaise for them both. Rob found a jug of homemade lemonade and poured two large glasses. He set them on the table and Liz slid into a chair, her stomach growling louder still at the sight of all the food.

"I think this is my favourite type of meal," she said.

He nodded, reaching for a cracker, and slicing off a chunk of brie to set on top of it. "Me too. Sometimes the bits and pieces make the best feasts."

"That's a great life motto," replied Liz with a laugh. "The bits and pieces make the best feasts. Perfect. That sums up the story of my life in a very succinct phrase. I had it all planned out, but the plan ended up costing me a lot of heartache. It was the little things along the way that have ended up meaning the most to me. Except my children, of course, they were always part of the plan, and having them, raising them, was the best thing I ever did."

Rob nodded, his eyes fixed on Liz's. "Me too. Jen is the only thing in my life I couldn't live without. Her and the grandchildren. Everything else is replaceable."

"Even your job?" asked Liz, then took a large bite of her sandwich. The flavours burst in her mouth, the lettuce adding a satisfying crunch.

He nodded, chewing. "If it came to that, I could give it up. It's become important to me, only because my life is so structured around it. But in the end, it's not the thing that brings me the most joy. Don't get me wrong, I love teaching. I thrive on bringing new ideas to the students, helping them to see things in different ways. It's satisfying, but it's not what makes my life worth living."

Liz swallowed. "You're absolutely right. I used to think my career was important, but then it all vanished in the blink of an eye, and I had no control over it. Cam decided to liquidate the business, and there wasn't a thing I could do about it. Everything I'd worked so hard to build, was so proud of, was gone just like that." She snapped her fingers in the air. Even saying the words out loud sent a pang through her gut. Since it happened, she hadn't wanted to speak much about it, avoided dealing fully with the pain of losing her life's work since it seemed insignificant next to the pain of losing her husband. But speaking the words brought a measure of release, her eyes stung with tears.

"Have you thought about what you'll do now?" he asked.

She inhaled a slow breath. "Yes. I think I'm finally ready to move on. Ready to start over. This trip has been good for me. You've been good for me." She smiled.

He took her hand in his, lifted it and played with her fingers, threading his through them, running his thumb in a circle around her palm.

She felt the air leave her lungs as a tingle ran down the length of her arm.

"I feel the same way about you," he replied.

Candlelight flickered over his face, the shadows lengthening across the kitchen floor as the heavy pummelling rain slowed.

"I can't believe..." Liz let the words hang in the air between them, her heart thundering.

"That we found each other, now. It seems so improbable after everything..." finished Rob.

He leaned toward her, closing the space between them, pressing his lips to hers. Liz's head spun as her eyes flickered shut. Rob's lips were soft against hers as he began a slow exploration. She shifted closer to him, slipping her arms around his neck. Their chairs clanked against one another. Rob stood, drawing her up with him. She pressed her body against his, lifting her head towards him, revelling in the scent of him, the strength of him, the strange but familiar caress of his lips on hers.

It was a time for second chances, for new beginnings, and the first blush of new love where barren hearts had ruled too long.

🐾 19 🐾

CABARITA BEACH

The noise of a magpie warbling outside his window woke Rob. He smiled and rolled onto his side, then sat up straight, stretching his arms over his head. Something about sleeping in a strange bed always gave him a crick in his neck. He shifted his head to one side, then the other, attempting to work out the knots with his fingertips, massaging the tired muscles.

He'd be back in his own bed that night. The thought didn't give him the satisfaction it usually would. After everything that'd happened the previous night with Liz, he was in no hurry to return to his life in Brisbane. After their kiss, they'd settled on the verandah until the power came back on, talking, laughing, and kissing until three o'clock in the morning. He couldn't remember the last time he'd done anything like it. Probably not since he was married at the age of twenty-two.

He chuckled at the memory, even as a pleasant warmth rushed through his body. Liz was certainly a unique woman. In the short time he'd known her, he'd developed feelings for her he hadn't experienced since Martha died a decade earlier. He'd been on dates in that time but hadn't found a woman who reminded him of his first love the way Liz did.

Rob stripped off his boxer shorts and stepped into the shower. The warm water beat down on his face and shoulders. He leaned against the wall with both hands, letting the spray massage the tension from his neck.

Truth be told, Liz and Martha couldn't be more different in most of the ways that people would notice, but there was still something about Liz that sparked recognition deep within him. She was gentle, yet strong, honest, and full of integrity. That much he could tell about her already. Characteristics shared by Martha.

On the surface, Martha was loud where Liz was quiet. The life of the party, his late wife's laughter could light up a room. While Liz drew attention with her poise and quiet confidence. In spite of their differences, Liz elicited feelings in Rob that'd died with Martha. Feelings he'd never thought would resurface, hadn't wanted to experience again for many years. But he was ready now.

Some people would say ten years was far too long, and his few remaining friends had confronted him lovingly on that very issue. But it'd taken him this long to deal with the pain of losing his wife and to ready himself for love again. Over the past year, he'd finally felt that he would be able to offer the kind of emotional connection a committed relationship required, yet hadn't met anyone who drew him in. Until, completely unexpectedly, along came Liz.

He switched off the shower and dried himself, then

dressed in a comfortable pair of shorts and a button-down shirt. He packed the few things he'd left out, into his suitcase and set it by the door. Then, stepped out of his room and glanced at Liz's door. Was it too soon to knock? It wasn't early, but after staying up so late, she might still be in bed asleep. It was eight-thirty in the morning, so she'd have to get up soon if they were to check-out of the inn by ten.

He rapped knuckles on the door and didn't get a response, then jogged down the stairs. The usual noise of breakfast preparation echoed from the kitchen and he smiled. At least they hadn't been forgotten this morning. He found Bindi by the reception desk.

"Good morning, Bindi," he said.

She faced him with a contrite smile. "I'm so sorry, Mr. Patch. We seemed to have had a few issues with our staffing schedule last night. Mrs. Cranwell told me no one showed up for the evening shift... I took the evening off, not feeling well, and Mima needed a rest. Still, there were supposed to be two staff on duty. Apparently, they each called and left a message on the machine, but of course no one was here to check for messages, so...." She shook her head.

"No worries at all, Bindi. We had a lovely evening and fended for ourselves quite nicely. These things happen from time to time." He grinned, offered her a mock salute, and wandered into the kitchen enticed by the smell of frying eggs.

"Mima, it smells divine in here. I wonder if I could convince you to move to Brisbane and cook for me every day?" he asked as he slid onto a stool beside the bench.

Mima chortled, her stomach shaking in time to her laughter. "Ah, Rob, aren't you a big old flirt? Are you asking me to move in with you? I'm afraid I'm a little old for you, my dear."

He laughed. "Another disappointment I shall have to bear. Though in all seriousness, I hope I will see you again. I've gotten used to being well taken care of. I'm afraid my dog isn't really up to the challenge, and I'll have to go back to a life of boring meals and one-sided conversations again."

She laughed. "Maybe, or maybe not. I have a feeling that things might be looking up..." Mima winked as Liz walked into the kitchen.

He stood and took Liz's hand in his, bent to kiss her cheek. His own warmed, and his heart rate accelerated at her touch.

"Good morning," he whispered against her hair. It tickled his skin and he resisted the urge to bury his head in its soft silkiness and kiss up and down her neck.

"Back at you." She smiled up at him.

"Breakfast is ready, you two," stated Mima with a grin. "It's still only the two of you, so I've made you a special assortment. And there'll be an onslaught of guests arriving before you know it, so enjoy the attention while it lasts." She winked and handed them each a plate of fried eggs, sourdough bread, bacon, mushrooms, and sliced fruit, fashioned into the shape of a half-moon.

❦

As they ate in the breakfast nook, Rob couldn't help wanting to be close to Liz. He sat beside her, leaned toward her, listened to everything she said. Almost as though he was a teenager all over again.

He'd called Jen several times the previous day before the power went out, but again she hadn't answered. He was still worried about her but knew he couldn't do anything until she made the choice herself. She'd asked him not to call the police a year ago when she'd finally called him back after failing to return his calls for over a week, so he was reluctant to do it now. He'd decided to try calling her again after breakfast, then he'd stop by her house on the way home. If he still hadn't been able to reach her before he headed to Brisbane, he'd call the police, whether she liked it or not.

Irritation buzzed through him. If only she'd call and let him know she was okay. His frustration was followed by fear, which he quickly pushed down. He couldn't think that way, it wouldn't help anyone. He focused his attention on Liz.

"What's wrong?" she asked, her brow furrowing with concern.

"I was thinking about Jen," he confessed.

"Any word yet?"

"No."

Liz inhaled a sharp breath. "That's not good. I hope nothing's wrong."

He hated to admit it, but there it was. His daughter hadn't gotten in touch with him after his repeated attempts to talk to her. Something was wrong.

"You don't think I'm being overprotective?"

She shook her head. "No, I don't. She should've called by now."

"I agree. I'm going to try again today, then go to the authorities."

"Okay."

She nodded, took another bite of mango.

"But let's not think about that now. It's going to steal my appetite, and I want to talk to you about something."

She quirked an eyebrow. "Oh?"

"Yes. Liz, this thing between us has taken me by surprise..."

She laughed. "Me too."

"I'm glad I'm not the only one." He leaned forward to kiss her softly on the lips. "And I wanted to ask you how you're feeling about it all... about us?"

Liz's lips pursed. "I'm feeling good."

He chuckled. "Right... well, that's a start."

"What about you?"

He thought for a moment about how to say it, how to express what he was feeling for the woman seated beside him who'd changed everything and stolen his heart in only a week. "I know we live in different cities, but I'd like to try to make things work between us."

She smiled. "I would too."

"Good. We're on the same track then."

She nodded. "I didn't think I'd find someone like you."

"Neither did I." He tucked a strand of hair behind her ear, then cupped her cheek with his hand.

She leaned into his palm, her eyes closing briefly. "I'm not sure it will work, though—with me in Dee Why and you in Brisbane."

His heart dropped. "I suppose you might be right..."

"You know, I don't have a job at the moment. My kids have left home, there's really nothing keeping me in Sydney. Maybe I should come to Brisbane, find a place to stay for a while... see where things take us."

His eyes widened. "You'd do that?"

She nodded. "I would... I don't want to miss out on the best things in life because I'm holding on too tight to the things I already have, things like my house, things that don't matter in the big scheme of things. Unless, you think it's too much, too fast..."

He shook his head, took her face between his hands, and kissed her passionately. "No, I'm speechless, but it's not too fast for me. I want to spend time with you, get to know you better, see if we can really make something of this."

"I do too."

"Then, it's settled. You're moving to Brisbane, at least for now."

She laughed. "I can't believe it, but yes—I'm moving to

Brisbane. I'll have to go home to pack up the house and get some things together to bring with me..."

"Of course... and while you're doing that I'll see if I can find a place in St. Lucia that might suit you."

"Perfect."

Mima cleared her throat, peering into the breakfast nook with wide eyes. Rob spun in his seat to face her. "Everything okay, Mima?"

She smiled. "Uh Rob, you have some visitors..."

Behind her, Jen stepped through the doorway with Daniel on one hip and Sophie clinging to her leg.

"Jen!" cried Rob, jumping up to embrace her.

Relief flooded through him as he kissed her cheek, then squeezed Daniel and lifted Sophie into his arms to kiss her little cheek as well.

"I can't believe you're here," he said, shaking his head. "You should've called. I've been worried about you. Come and sit down, we're eating breakfast, but you're welcome to mine if you like... are you hungry?"

Jen sighed, slid into a chair, setting Daniel's feet on the ground. "No, we ate already. Thanks Dad. I'm sorry I didn't call, but I didn't have a chance. I left him, Dad. I left him." Her eyes flooded with tears.

"You did?" He lowered himself into the chair beside her, squeezing her arm with one hand. "I'm glad."

"I can't process it all yet, but I packed our bags and slipped out of the house while he was in the shower. It didn't give us much time, but it was all the time I needed."

"I'm glad you're here." He wanted to know why she had to wait until her husband was in the shower to get away. Why she felt so trapped in her marriage, in her own home. What Neil had done to her, to the kids, but those questions could wait. Today, it was enough that she was here, that she'd made the choice to walk away from the toxic relationship he'd been hoping she'd leave behind for years.

"It's nice to see you again, Jen," said Liz.

He stood. "Jen, you remember Liz?"

Jen nodded, smiled. "Oh, yes hi, Liz. It's nice to see you too. I'm sorry, my head is spinning, I can't think straight right now."

"That's understandable," replied Liz. "And no need to apologise."

"Dad, do you think we could go to your room to rest for a few minutes before we drive to Brisbane?" asked Jen, looking suddenly tired.

He patted her arm. "Of course. Come on, I'll take you upstairs. We've still got a little while before check-out. Then, we'll go home."

He led Jen and the children to his room, then hurried back downstairs to where Liz was finishing up her final cup of tea. She was staring out the long, rectangular windows that lined the walls of the breakfast nook when he walked through the door. Sunlight glanced off the silverware, leaving a rainbow reflection on the wall.

He sat across from Liz with a sigh. "Sorry for the interruption."

"I don't mind at all. I'm glad that Jen and the kids are safe. Now you can stop worrying about them."

"Not sure a parent ever really stops worrying. Do they?" he quipped with a wink.

She laughed. "You're right about that."

"Still, I'm relieved she's here. And I hope it sticks."

"You think she'll go back to him?" asked Liz.

He shrugged. "Who knows." He leaned forward to kiss her softly across the table, then took her hands in his. "So, this is goodbye for now. I have to get the family to Brisbane before Neil comes here, looking for them."

She nodded. "Yes, of course. I'll see you soon."

Another kiss, this one lingered longer. He hated to say goodbye; he wanted to spend the day together, but she'd be in Brisbane soon, and they could spend every day getting to know one another. He kissed her one last time, then waved goodbye, imprinting her smile in his mind's eye as he walked away.

❧ 20 ☙

3RD APRIL 1996

SAINT LUCIA, QLD

A candle in the centre of the table flickered in the dim lighting. The jazz quartet in the corner of the restaurant offered a soothing score to underwrite the romantic setting. Liz reached for Rob's hand across the table and rested her own on top of it. He turned his hand over and wove his fingers through hers. Her heart was full.

"I finished unpacking my boxes today," she said. "I honestly didn't think it would take me so long, but it's been busy since I moved here."

He laughed. "I know what you mean. It's hard to believe you've been here two months already."

"Time flies..."

"When you're falling in love," finished Rob with a wink.

She chuckled. "I had no idea you were so corny."

He shrugged. "I'm full of surprises."

"Well, thank you for this wonderful dinner. I'm absolutely chock-full. I couldn't eat another bite... unless of course the dessert menu looks good."

"I'm not big on dessert, but I've eaten here before, and it's pretty amazing."

She sighed. "In that case, I suppose I'll have to wait a few minutes to make room. It's such a hardship."

He laughed. "I thought this would be a good way to celebrate you finishing your unpacking and closing on your first contract with a local developer. It's amazing how quickly you've landed on your feet and embraced Brisbane."

"I love it here already. Although, I do miss my friends..."

"I know you do. That's another reason I wanted to share this meal together. There are a few things I want to talk to you about."

Their waitress stopped by the table with a smile, her hands clasping two menus in front of black slacks and a white button-down shirt. "Would you like to see the dessert menu?" she asked.

Liz nodded. "I would. Thank you." She took the menu and scanned the items listed. "I'll have the chocolate brownie with ice cream, and a cappuccino, please."

Rob ordered a chai tea, then shifted his chair closer so he could hold Liz's hands, their knees bumping together.

"The past few months have been some of the happiest of my life. Having Jen and the kids living with me, then you joining us in a house down the street. I've fallen completely, head over heels in love with you, Liz."

She smiled, reaching up a hand to stroke his cheek. "I feel the same way."

"I want to spend the rest of my life with you. Will you marry me?'

Liz's breath caught in her throat. That wasn't what she'd been expecting him to say. Not yet. It was so soon; they were getting to know each other. They weren't young anymore, and both had children. Their lives were complicated.

"Marry you?" she squeaked.

He nodded. "I know it's sudden, and it's fast, but I also know you're the one. I want to be clear about where we're going. We can take our time with the engagement, but I want to be heading towards marriage, to be a family."

Her throat tightened and tears filled her eyes. "Yes, I'll marry you."

He kissed her then, with a passion and love that sent sparks shooting through her body, warming her from head to toe.

When he pulled back, he tugged something from his pants pocket and set it on the table. It was a black jewellery box. He flicked it open and reached for the ring that was nestled in a small velvet cushion. She gasped at the sight of the ornate ring, with an old-fashioned setting, small diamonds around a single large stone.

"It's beautiful," she whispered.

He grinned. "I found it at an antique shop and thought it suited you perfectly—it's stylish and classic all at the same time."

A tear wound its way down her cheek. He knew her better than she'd realised. And despite her surprise at his proposal, she'd known for weeks they'd get married someday. She didn't expect it would be so soon.

He kissed her again.

The desserts arrived and he pushed his chair back to the other side of the small, square table. Liz couldn't stop smiling. She stared down at the ring through glimmering tears, turning it one way, then the other, watching as the candlelight reflected off the diamonds.

She took a bite of the brownie but couldn't think about anything other than the surprise proposal and their engagement. She was engaged. Even thinking the words felt strange but exhilarating all at the same time. The girls wouldn't believe it when she told them. Or the kids.

Her heart skipped a beat. What would her children say?

She inhaled a slow breath. It was her life. They'd be happy for her. It'd be fine. Better than fine, it would be fantastic.

Rob took a sip of tea. "There's something else I wanted to talk to you about as well."

She nodded. "Okay. I hope it's not bigger than the proposal, or my heart might not survive this meal." She chuckled.

He pursed his lips. "Maybe now isn't the time."

She set her spoon on the table, her eyes wide. "It's bigger than a proposal?"

He shook his head. "No, I don't think so, but it's a significant life change... if we decide together it's what we want to do."

Liz steeled herself with a quick breath. "Let's discuss it then. I don't think I could forget it now that you've brought it up. I'll spend all night staring at the ceiling wondering what you wanted to talk about."

He smiled. "Okay. Well, as you know, Jen and the kids are doing well living with me. The kids have settled into their new schools, they're happy, and adjusting to their new lives."

She nodded. "They're doing really well."

"But Neil is still causing trouble."

Her nose wrinkled. "Yes, he is. I'm not sure what we can do about it. You've spoken with the police several times. They said they couldn't do anything."

He quirked an eyebrow. "Exactly. So, I've secretly been talking to the dean of the science department at Sydney Uni. He's offered me a position teaching biology."

Liz gaped. "What?"

"It's not settled, I haven't accepted his offer. I wanted to talk to you about it first. What do you think? We could move to Sydney, you'd be back with your friends, Jen and the kids could put some distance between them and Neil..."

"It's a great idea," said Liz, her heart swelling. She could go home, be in her own house again, see her friends. It was more than she could've dreamed of. By accepting Rob's proposal, she'd believed she was turning away from all of that forever.

"So, you think we should do it?"

She nodded. "I think we should..." She squealed and stood, threw her arms around his neck, and kissed him hard on the mouth. "Thank you!"

He laughed. "I'm glad you're happy about it. It'll be an adjustment for me, but I think this is the perfect time for a fresh start. We'll be married, Jen and the kids will be free, and we can embark on a brand-new adventure together."

EPILOGUE

CABARITA BEACH

Rob stepped out of his car, locked it, and walked into the Waratah Inn. It wasn't cold like it'd been in Sydney when they'd bundled up at Liz's house to head to the airport. He had to admit; her house was magnificent. She'd put so much thought into every detail of the expansive property. He was glad she hadn't sold it when she moved to Brisbane. Every item of furniture, every knickknack spoke of her beauty, her poise, her stylish attention to detail. No wonder she was such a sought-after architect. Ever since they'd moved to Sydney and she'd put out feelers to her old clients, she'd had more work than she could manage. Her new business was already making waves in the architectural community.

He opened the door, stepped over the threshold, then listened. Sounds of laughter, children's voices raised in argument echoed out to greet him.

Inside, the noise rose as he moved through the inn to the kitchen. He found Liz in the kitchen, slipping chocolate chip biscuits from a tray onto a plate. Mima stood beside her, apron tight around her waist, a wide smile on her lips. Behind Mima, Kate, the chef at the inn, buzzed around basting things and stirring pots. He greeted them both.

Rob wrapped his arms around Liz, spun her in place to face him, and kissed her.

She smiled against his lips. "There you are future husband. How was it saying goodbye to your colleagues?"

He pressed his forehead to hers, staring into her eyes, kissed the tip of her nose. Then he released her to reach for a biscuit. It was hot and burned the tips of his fingers.

"Ah, still hot!" he whispered.

She laughed. "That will teach you to wait." She handed him a clean plate, and he set the biscuit on it and slid into a chair.

"It was hard to say farewell. It's a wonderful department, but I'm so excited to move on and get stuck into the research I'll be doing at Sydney Uni."

"I'm so glad, honey. Everyone will be arriving for tea soon, so if you could help me keep track of them all, that would be great."

He nodded. On Saturday they'd be married, and everyone was gathering at the Waratah Inn for the wedding. The rest of the week promised plenty of food, friends, family, and utter bedlam. Just exactly what he and Liz both loved and had been lacking for so many years they were almost giddy with excitement over it. He loved the way she was such a perfect match for him.

There was a noise at the front door. Liz handed him the plate of biscuits. "These are for your grandchildren. I'll see who's at the door."

Bindi strode toward the door and Liz followed her, falling

into an easy conversation with the inn's manager. Their laughter floated back to him.

He smiled, took a bite of his biscuit, then headed for the back door. Sophie and Daniel were playing in the backyard. Jen stood behind Daniel, watching them both.

"Mum, look a ladybird! Look!" he cried.

She laughed. "Wow, I wonder where she's going."

Rob set the plate on the outdoor table. "Biscuits! Get them while they're hot."

Both kids scurried to the table.

Rob laughed. "Anyone would think the two of you hadn't been fed in days."

Jen followed them, kissed him on the cheek, and wound an arm around his waist. "How'd it go at the office?"

He sighed. "After a small and very sedate departmental farewell party, I collected my box of things and shut the door on my empty office. It's amazing how so many years of study, research and teaching can be scooped up into one small box and an enormous collection of floppy disks." He chuckled. "And even though it was a little sad, as I walked away, I thought about my new beginnings instead of the past I'm leaving behind. Then, I felt much better."

She inhaled a deep breath. "I'm proud of you, Dad. It isn't easy to leave everything behind and start afresh."

His throat tightened. It was a strange feeling to have his child say those words, he told her so often how proud he was of her, but it wasn't the kind of thing he expected to hear her say to him.

"Thank you, sweetheart. I'm proud of you as well. We're both starting over. I'm glad we'll be close by, not sure if I could've made the move if I was leaving you and the kids behind as well."

She smiled, her eyes glistening. "I'm nervous about the move, but I know we'll figure things out as we go. And I'm so grateful to you for buying us a place to live. I promise, it won't be forever. I'll get back on my feet again and pay my own way..."

He shook his head. "Please, I wanted to do it. I sold my house in St Lucia and had to invest the money somewhere. I'm moving into Liz's house, so I don't need it. You do need it. Voila! And you'd inherit it from me one day anyway... I don't want you to move out. I want you to stay there. Think of it as your home. When you find a job, and there's no rush, you'll have plenty of things to spend the money on. This is something I want to do for you."

She rested her head on his chest with a sob. "Thank you, Dad. I don't know how to thank you enough. I'm so sorry for what I've put you through."

He kissed the top of her head. "You haven't put me through anything. None of this was your fault. And there's no point dwelling on the past, this is a new beginning for all of us."

Jen met his gaze with a smile. "I'm glad you're happy. Liz is wonderful."

He nodded. "Thank you, and I agree—she is."

The back door opened, and Liz stepped through it. Behind her, a young man and woman, both with blonde hair, followed.

"Rob, Jen, these are my children, David and Danita."

Liz stood on the edge of the beach. A cold wind ruffled the hem of her dress and lifted the loose tendrils of hair from the back of her neck, making her shiver. The cove behind the inn sparkled and glinted in the sunlight.

She'd chosen a winter wedding at the beach, but the cool air was making her rethink the choice. Still, it was a stunning day. They sky was a perfect shade of deep blue, without a single cloud in sight. The sand shimmered golden beneath the sun's soft rays, and gentle waves curled along the shore, splashing and sighing on the black rocky outcropping at the end of the beach.

She tugged her faux fur white shrug a little tighter around her shoulders, grateful at least for its warmth. The pale pink silk dress she wore did nothing to stop the cool breeze.

Beside her, her father stood, dressed in a navy suit with no tie and bare feet. She wiggled her own bare toes in the sand, grateful to see the pink nail polish was still intact.

Her father smiled, lifting a hand in her direction with an arched eyebrow. "Ready to go?" he asked.

She nodded. "Ready."

She slipped her arm through his and together they walked down the narrow path to the beach. She and her parents had never been particularly close, but she was grateful for their presence on her wedding today. Her father's calm helped to soothe her nerves.

Ahead of her, in the sand, rows of white seats were set out side by side. A white archway covered in a pink climbing vine stood behind the reverend who'd be officiating their wedding. Next to him, she saw Rob. The nerves that'd been buzzing in her stomach faded when her eyes rested on his kind face.

As she strode along the beach, soft music issued from a boom box on a white table beside the rows of chairs. The sound was thin in the giant, open space of the beach. The noise of the ocean almost drowned it out, but it was how Liz had wanted it to be. They'd fallen in love to the soundtrack of waves thundering onto the sandy shoreline, it was fitting they'd be married to the same tune.

They'd decided not to have bridesmaids or groomsmen, though Margot and Ivy had both declared themselves brides-maids in any case and had made sure to do everything a good bridesmaid should. They were seated in the front row and stood with the rest of the small crowd as Liz reached the makeshift aisle. Seated behind them, Mima, Bindi, Kate, Alex and Jack fairly gleamed in their Sunday best. Jack's grey hair, unencumbered by his usual Akubra hat, was slicked to one side. Bindi wore a green sheath dress with a matching jacket that fit her slim figure perfectly. Mima beamed and offered Liz a wink. Margot and Ivy sniffled into handkerchiefs and blinked back the tears.

Liz grinned, feeling her throat tighten at the sight of tears in her friends' eyes.

By the time she'd reached Rob's side, she was fighting to keep her emotions in check. A year ago, she'd never have imagined she'd be standing here, with a wonderful man about to pledge his life to her. She'd seen a future of lonely days, empty nights, and old age looming without anyone to share it with. But that was behind her now.

Rob took her hands in his, a wide grin splitting his face in two. She couldn't help smiling at his obvious delight.

The reverend led them in their short vows, then announced that Rob could kiss his bride. To the sound of hoots and laughter from the audience, he bent Liz backwards and planted a large smooch on her lips, then pulled her to her feet again, wrapped his arms around her and kissed her passionately.

She pulled away from him finally, laughing.

His eyes glowed. "You're the most beautiful bride in the world, Mrs. Patch."

"Thank you, Mr. Patch."

They walked hand in hand down the aisle, kissing and welcoming everyone who'd come to celebrate with them. When they were done, everyone followed them back to the inn where Kate had thrown together a lavish feast of seafood and salads, along with every type of dessert imaginable—

pavlovas with fresh cream and slices of fruit, lemon meringue pie, apple pie, custard, and Rob's favourite-chocolate self-saucing pudding.

They ate together and talked about the future, laughed together over the past and shared from the heart.

Liz made sure Rob didn't leave her side, holding tight to his hand. She couldn't be happier and now that the ceremony was over, she felt nothing but joy and peace over the prospect of a life spent together.

Seated side by side on the couch, she leaned toward him, kissed his cheek, and whispered in his ear. "Thank you for finding me."

He chuckled. "Right back at you."

She glanced around the room, her heart swelling at the sights and sounds of the inn, the place where they'd met and fallen in love at Christmas, filled with family, friends, and the love she'd wished to have for so many years. She knew the future wouldn't be perfect, that they'd face challenges. But they'd face them together. She wouldn't have to do it alone. And the thought comforted her, filled the empty spaces that'd taken up residence in her heart, and overwhelmed her with peace.

THE END

ALSO BY LILLY MIRREN

The Waratah Inn

Wrested back to Cabarita Beach by her grandmother's sudden death, Kate Summer discovers a mystery buried in the past that changes everything.

One Summer in Italy

Reeda leaves the Waratah Inn and returns to Sydney, her husband, and her thriving interior design business, only to find her marriage in tatters. She's lost sight of what she wants in life and can't recognise the person she's become.

The Summer Sisters

Set against the golden sands and crystal clear waters of Cabarita Beach three sisters inherit an inn and discover a mystery about their grandmother's past that changes everything they thought they knew about their family...

Christmas at The Waratah Inn

Liz Cranwell is divorced and alone at Christmas. When

her friends convince her to holiday at The Waratah Inn, she's dreading her first Christmas on her own. Instead she discovers that strangers can be the balm to heal the wounds of a lonely heart in this heartwarming Christmas story.

ABOUT THE AUTHOR

Lilly Mirren lives in Brisbane, Australia with her husband and three children.

Lilly always dreamed of being a writer and is now living that dream. She is a graduate of both the University of Queensland, where she studied International Relations and Griffith University, where she completed a degree in Information Technology.

When she's not writing, she's chasing her children, doing housework or spending time with friends.

Lilly is also a bestselling sweet romance author under the pen name *Vivi Holt*.

Sign up for her newsletter and stay up on all the latest Lilly book news.

And follow her on:

Website: lillymirren.com
Facebook: https://www.facebook.com/authorlillymirren/
Twitter: https://twitter.com/lilly_mirren
BookBub: https://www.bookbub.com/authors/lilly-mirren

Made in the USA
Coppell, TX
11 March 2020

16709066R00115